6 Chelsea Walk

This series is a unique collaboration between three
award-winning authors, Adèle Geras, Linda Newbery
and Ann Turnbull, all writing about one very special
house and the extraordinary girls and women who
have lived there throughout history.

6 Chelsea Walk

1895

Girls
behind the
Camera

ADÈLE GERAS

USBORNE

For Finn, Colm and Marcella Keating

This edition published 2018. First published in 2007 as "Historical House: Cecily's Portrait" by Usborne Publishing Ltd., Usborne House, 83-85 Saffron Hill, London EC1N 8RT, England.
www.usborne.com

Copyright © Adèle Geras, 2007.

A CIP catalogue record for this book is available from the British Library.

JFMAM JASOND/18   00988/5   ISBN: 9781474954976

Printed in the UK.

Contents

6 Chelsea Walk, 1895

Basement

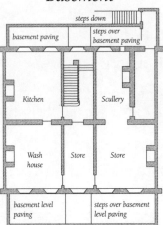

steps down

basement paving

steps over basement paving

Kitchen

Scullery

Wash house

Store

Store

basement level paving

steps over basement level paving

First-floor

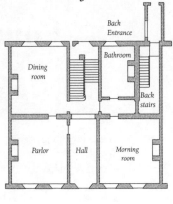

Back Entrance

Bathroom

Dining room

Back stairs

Parlor

Hall

Morning room

Second-floor

Library

Bathroom

Back stairs

Drawing room

Disused room

Mr. Bright's bedroom

Third-floor

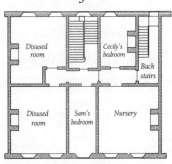

Disused room

Cecily's bedroom

Back stairs

Disused room

Sam's bedroom

Nursery

Roof space

Florrie's bedroom

Nanny Mildred's bedroom

Back stairs

Attic

Cook's bedroom

CHAPTER ONE

Ghosts

Cecily Bright and her friend Amy Chistlehurst had come home from school and were sitting in the nursery of Number Six, Chelsea Walk, talking about whether the house might be haunted.

"I've lived here all my life," said Cecily, "and that's twelve years. Papa was born in this house nearly forty years ago, in 1857, and he's never seen a ghost either."

"Have you asked him?" Amy wanted to know.

"Perhaps he *has* seen one and doesn't want to frighten you by saying so. You say your papa told you it was a school for young ladies more than a hundred years ago... If the house has been lived in for so long, *someone* must have died here during all that time."

"Schoolgirls don't die while they're at school. Or at least, I've never heard of such a thing." Cecily looked away. "But my mother did...she died upstairs in her bedroom."

Amy's eyes widened and she put a hand over her mouth as if she wanted to stop the sound coming out, but it was too late. The dreadful words, the ones she ought never to have uttered, had been spoken.

"I didn't think!" Amy turned scarlet with shame and ran to hug Cecily. "It just slipped out of my mouth before I could stop it...oh, I'm sorry. Will you *ever* forgive me, Cecily? I'm so thoughtless. Please say you're still my friend. I'd hate not to come here and play with you. Imagine if we couldn't see one another whenever we liked! How would I escape my brothers and sisters?"

"You're forgiven," Cecily said. "Though I don't think you should speak so about your family. You're lucky to have them all. We rattle around in this big house, Papa says. Just him and me and Sam… Since Mama died, it's been very empty and quiet." She smiled at Amy. "I wish there *were* such a thing as a ghost in this house. I wish my mama would come back."

"Only restless spirits return." Amy sounded very sure of herself. "Your mother must be at peace."

Cecily thought that being at peace sounded very pleasant. She herself was always, even at her happiest, aware of the fact that she had no mother and this meant that there was a little grief mixed in with everything she felt. She also knew that Papa was lonely, however much she tried to be a companion to him and no matter how often he told her that he was perfectly content.

John Bright worked as a clerk in lawyers' chambers, near St. Paul's Cathedral. He had friends with whom he went for walks sometimes, or who occasionally came to Number Six to play cards. He even had what Nanny Mildred called "a lady friend", whose name was Ellen Braithwaite. She was the sister of a colleague of Papa's and whenever Cecily thought of her, she felt her spirits drop. Miss Braithwaite was not plain, but not pretty either. She wore clothes in colours that weren't colours at all, in Cecily's opinion: grey and fawn and dun and shades of red and blue that were so dark you could hardly tell them apart from black. Miss Braithwaite wasn't very talkative, nor was she altogether silent. She was of medium height, had light brown hair which she wore done up behind her head in a round bun and was in every way completely unremarkable. She shared Papa's interest in exploration and the study of nature and all the latest scientific discoveries. Whenever she came to the house, they spent a great deal of time in the study, poring over maps and charts and she helped him to arrange and classify his small collection of fossils. Cecily could tell that Miss Braithwaite was devoted to Papa and she feared that

Papa might grow used to her and perhaps even fall in love with her and ask her to marry him. She decided to confide in Amy.

"You remember Miss Braithwaite?"

Amy nodded. "I have seen her often and she's just as you describe her."

"I fear she may fall in love with Papa. She might even persuade him to marry her."

"Never!" Amy said. She sounded very confident, and Cecily was relieved. Amy went on: "Miss Ellen Braithwaite sounds extremely dull, as well as looking quite plain. Your papa is far too clever to marry such a person. And my mama says gentlemen like pretty ladies. Miss Braithwaite cannot be called pretty, so there is no need for you to worry."

"But they like the same things."

"One likes the same things as many people and yet one doesn't fall in love with them. Love is..." Amy sought for the right words. "Love is mysterious and unfathomable."

Cecily thought that perhaps her friend was quoting from one of the romances to which Mrs. Chistlehurst was devoted, but she allowed herself to be reassured. She'd dreamed of her father marrying again, and while she'd often imagined the ceremony and had even drawn sketches of the dress she might wear, she was not sure she would be happy if someone else came to live in the house with them. Mama had gone, but if Papa married again, his new bride would certainly want to be their mother, hers and Sam's. That was out of the question, for no one could take Mama's place.

Mary Bright died after Samuel, Cecily's little brother, was born. She fell ill with a fever after the birth and within two days she had gone for ever, leaving Papa and Cecily alone with a tiny baby to care for. Aunt Lizzie, who was now Cecily's favourite person in the whole world after Papa and Sam, had taken leave from her work in Sussex, where she was a gardener for a family who lived in a fine mansion. She'd moved in at once to help them. Grandmother Findlay, Mama's mother, travelled to London for her only daughter's funeral, but returned to her chilly house straight afterwards. She was old and infirm now and the Brights rarely went to visit her, in her house near Edinburgh. Cecily found her a difficult person to like, even though she was a relation. When Cecily first met Amy, she realized what a very small family she and Sam had in comparison with other people, though perhaps the Chistlehursts, with their abundance of aunts and uncles and cousins, were a little unusual themselves.

In any case, Aunt Lizzie was the best aunt in the world and Cecily would not have exchanged her for a brace of other relatives. She stayed for a few weeks after the funeral and the first thing she did was hire Nanny Mildred to look after the children and be a housekeeper to Papa. Florrie, the nursery maid, was a young girl when she came to help Nanny, and now that Cecily and Sam were a little older, she was a maid of all work. Together with Cook, Nanny and Florrie looked after the house and the family, and Cecily was grateful for their presence.

"Mama was the prettiest person in the world," Cecily told Amy. "When she died, I was only six. That's how old Sam is now, and he seems such a baby still."

Cecily could remember how the house had looked and felt just after Mama's death. What she would never forget – what was still there even now if you knew where to look for it – was the sadness everywhere, which seemed to take up the space that used to be filled with laughter and the sound of happy voices. Papa became suddenly much quieter. He was kind to her even when he must have been as sad as sad himself. She could recall going into the bedroom to see the new baby, when Mama was ill. How pale she'd been! Her skin was almost the same colour as the pillows.

Cecily shivered. She said to Amy, "I do know what Mama looked like, of course, but it's becoming harder and harder to remember everything and sometimes I have to look at the picture in the drawing room before I can bring her face to mind."

There was one daguerreotype of her father and her mother on their wedding day in the front parlour. Cecily sometimes stared at this picture, trying to match up her memories of her mother with the pretty, but somehow stiff and formal-looking person in the frame.

"Even when I look at her portrait," she went on, "it's not exactly her. I remember how happy I used to feel when she laughed and played with me and I think of her every night before I go to sleep and then sometimes…"

"Sometimes what?" Amy prompted her friend.

"Nothing. Let's play with the doll's house."

"But I have to go now, Cecily." Amy sighed. "I promised Mama I would be home early today."

"Then I'll see you at school tomorrow."

Amy ran down the stairs to the front door and Cecily waved from the landing. Then she went into the nursery again. She'd been about to tell Amy that she sometimes fancied she could feel Mama's lips soft on her forehead; her hands smoothing the eiderdown. And I think I can hear her voice, Cecily told herself, and the songs she used to sing to lull me to sleep. Perhaps it was a good thing she hadn't mentioned that to Amy. It would only have set off more talk of ghosts.

I'm lucky, she thought, that Amy lives next door. The Chistlehursts were the nearest thing to the family in *Little Women* that Cecily had ever met. This book, by Miss Louisa May Alcott, was a great favourite of both girls and Amy had indeed been named after the Amy in the novel, though she agreed with Cecily that Jo was easily the best of the four March sisters. Amy was, unlike her namesake, the eldest of four children. She was very pretty, like her fictional counterpart, though not as vain. She had no intention of putting a clothes peg on her nose while she slept to improve it and coax it into a more fashionable shape. She was small and dainty, too, and Cecily (who was tall and not at all dainty and had red-gold hair which fell down her back in a riot of curls when it wasn't bound up in plaits for school), felt large and awkward next to her. Amy had two younger brothers called Albert and Edmund, and a baby sister called Daisy. It fell to her, she always told Cecily, to look after these little ones far more than was fair.

Amy also had a mother and father who were both alive and well and seemingly happy to live in the untidy and, according to Nanny Mildred, "rather rackety" household next door to the Brights. Amy and Cecily had met at school and because both of them liked the same lessons and laughed at the same things, they became friends at once. Amy was braver than Cecily, and was also very good at thinking of exciting games to play, which often involved dressing up and acting.

Cecily was crouching on the floor of the nursery, thinking how lucky she was to have such a good friend and happily rearranging the furniture in her doll's house, when the door flew open and Sam ran in, weeping. She sighed. Cecily couldn't ignore her little brother when he was so distressed. He was making a great deal of noise with his sobbing. Should she remind him of his pocket handkerchief before he dragged his sleeve across his very damp face? Perhaps not. Instead, Cecily stood up and gathered Sam into her arms.

"Stop crying," she said, "and tell me what's happened."

CHAPTER TWO

Mossy is Missing

"Mossy's lost. I've called her and called her and she won't come."

Mossy was Sam's new kitten. Cecily knew that even though the pretty little black and white cat had been a present from their father to Sam at Christmas a few weeks ago, she was the one who was really in charge of Mossy's welfare. Sam loved her, but he sometimes forgot to go down to the kitchen and remind Cook that it was feeding time. Cook said she was far too busy to worry about a cat and whether or not she ate her meals regularly.

"A cat must earn its keep by eating mice," she said, sniffing a little at the inconvenience of having two children getting under her feet. But Cecily knew that no mouse could possibly be as tasty as the morsels of meat from the Sunday roast which she had to cut up into very small pieces. Sam was too young to handle the knife. He didn't mind his sister helping with the care of Mossy, and Cecily had more patience than her brother when it came to sitting still and reading her book quietly whenever the kitten decided that a lap was just the place for a long sleep. And now Sam's darling…her darling, too…was lost.

"When did you last see her?"

"A long time ago. Let's go and look outside. Maybe she's run away down the road. I think she has, Cecily."

"Why do you think that? Mossy doesn't like the cold and there's snow on the ground today."

Sam hung his head and wept even more noisily. "I opened the door. I wanted to go and make a snowball. I think Mossy ran out. I tried to stop her."

"You think? Aren't you sure? Come, Sam, tell me the truth. I won't help you unless you tell me exactly what happened."

Sam *had* let Mossy out. Cecily stood up. There was nothing for it. They'd have to go and ask permission from Nanny Mildred to go and look for her.

"Maybe," Sam said, "Mossy's found a door open and run into the warm?"

"We'll have to knock at every house and ask if they've seen her. Let's go and tell Nanny and fetch our coats and outdoor shoes."

Nanny Mildred had given the children strict instructions. They weren't to knock too loudly on doors; they were to introduce themselves very politely, say clearly where they lived and ask whether Mossy had been seen. If she had not, then they were allowed to ask whoever they were addressing to keep an eye out for the silly creature. "Silly creature" was what Nanny often called Mossy, and Cecily saw that Sam frowned whenever he heard her say those words.

"And," Nanny added, "you must remember to say *thank you* as you leave. No one likes strange children appearing out of the blue. They might think you were up to mischief. I shouldn't like that. No, indeed. I rely on you, Cecily, to take care of your brother."

"Yes, Nanny," Cecily said. "We'll be very good, I promise." Cecily took her brother's hand as they left Number Six. She noticed that however worried he may have been about Mossy, he still managed to enjoy brushing the piled-up snow from the black iron of the railings near the gate.

The snow had fallen yesterday. It was far too late for such cold weather in Cecily's opinion. February the fifteenth was almost springtime, she thought, but here was the snow, making all the trees sparkle as though white diamonds had been scattered through the branches. The cold, glittering stuff crunched under their boots as they made their way along Chelsea Walk. Usually, whenever they went anywhere together, Sam never stopped talking and asking questions but he was silent now. It was nearly three o'clock and soon the sky, which was already mauve and darkening, would be quite black and the street lights would be on. They had to make sure, Nanny Mildred said, to be back before Papa returned home from his work.

Cecily was used to being the person who looked after Sam, and she was careful never to tell anyone how she wished that there was someone to look after her. If we had a mother, she thought, as they peered into every front garden, looking for what might be a kitten's footprints, *she*'d be out here with Sam instead of me. I'd be upstairs in the nursery still, with the da Pontes. Mama had given Cecily the dolls for her sixth birthday and she'd named them all before she died. They were called after the da Ponte family whom Mama and Papa had met while they were on their honeymoon in Venice, before Cecily was born. Mama had told her all about them and even though Cecily had been younger than Sam was now, she remembered every word. The da Pontes were bakers. Papa and Mama da Ponte had a little boy called Paolo and a little girl who was Magdalena, or Maggie for short, and they also had a baby whose name Mama couldn't recall. It had been Mama's idea to call her Bambina. This meant "little girl" in Italian. It was also Mama who suggested that a house for the dolls to live in would be a delightful addition to the nursery, and the wood for making it had arrived in the house before she became ill.

After Mama died, Papa began to make the doll's house for Cecily. He put it together all by himself, hammering the wood late at night, down in the basement of the house. Then, when it was finished, he brought it upstairs, to the nursery. Cecily had helped her father to decorate each room. She'd chosen the papers for the walls and Papa had cut and pasted them to the wood. There were so many beautiful patterns to choose from and Cecily finally decided on a paper (designed by Mr. Walter Crane, who was a famous artist and wallpaper designer, much admired by Mama) with parakeets and pomegranates on it for the doll's house drawing room, and one covered in cabbage roses for the bedrooms. The five da Pontes lived there very happily. She'd been about to put Bambina da Ponte into her new cradle when Sam came bursting into the room with the news of Mossy's disappearance.

Cecily wondered whether it was true that because she was twelve, she was too old to be playing with dolls. Twelve, she'd begun to realize, was a strange sort of age to be. Her teachers, her father, Nanny Mildred and every adult she knew didn't seem able to make up their minds about it. Sometimes it was: "Oh, Cecily, you're much too grown up for that," and then "*that*" was things like playing with her dolls, crying too easily when she felt sad, or being frightened to go to sleep without a nightlight. But sometimes it was "No,

Cecily, you're much too young for that!" Then "*that*" became things like, for example, riding on the omnibus with Amy to visit the Science Museum. You needed a grown-up to go with you…you were too young. You were too young, also, to overhear conversations between adults, though she and Amy had managed to pick up a great deal of information when their elders weren't paying attention. When Amy came to visit, Cecily quite liked arranging the dolls around their dining table and pretending they were grand society folk having dinner parties and love affairs, but Amy soon tired of these games and persuaded her friend to do something more interesting, like playing at ladies and maids. Or practising writing love letters for when they fell in love, which would be quite soon, she felt sure. Or pasting scraps into a large scrapbook, or writing long plays full of murder and passion and then acting them out. Or, as she had this afternoon, trying to persuade her to go ghost-hunting in the rooms on the second floor of Number Six.

Cecily had never explained to anyone why she loved her doll's house so much. It had been the one thing that had lifted her grief a little in the days after Mama died. The times that she and Papa had spent together on the floor of the nursery as he put the final touches to the doll's house were the least terrible times of the terrible days after Mama's funeral. She and Papa used to talk about the dolls. "Look at this wardrobe," he said one day. "The da Pontes will hang all their fine clothes in it."

"They don't have any fine clothes, Papa. Only what they're wearing."

"Then we'll ask your Aunt Lizzie to make them all the clothes they will need, never fear."

Remembering this, Cecily smiled. Her Aunt Lizzie was Papa's older sister. It was Aunt Lizzie who'd planted the walnut that was now a big tree in the back garden. Cecily liked hearing the story about how ill Papa had been when he was a tiny baby. He'd nearly died and the day that he got better was the very day

Aunt Lizzie noticed that her walnut had put out its first green shoot.

It was their great good fortune, Papa had told Cecily, that they could still live here, in this fine house. It used to belong to Papa and Aunt Lizzie's Uncle Percy, and Papa's Cousin Hugh should have inherited the property after his father's death. But poor Cousin Hugh died himself, in India, of a fever caught while he was climbing a very high mountain looking for a particularly unusual variety of butterfly. Cousin Clara, who'd been a nurse for many years and was now retired and living with her family in Scotland, had no desire to move back to London and Cousin Lucy had gone to live in Italy with her husband, who was a wealthy and aristocratic Italian gentleman. According to Aunt Lizzie, Cousin Lucy would not have considered marrying anyone who wasn't wealthy and aristocratic. And so the house, which was really much too large for Papa and Cecily and Sam, was theirs for as long as they wanted it. Some of the upstairs rooms were closed up, and even though Nanny Mildred said they'd come in useful when visitors came, Aunt Lizzie was the only person who ever stayed overnight, as far as Cecily could tell. The furniture in these rooms was swathed in white dust sheets and Cecily avoided them for the most part. Sometimes, though, when Amy came to play, the two girls opened a door and went in to explore in secret, as they had today. Nanny Mildred would not have been pleased to know about these visits and Cecily was always relieved when they went back to the nursery.

Aunt Lizzie lived in Sussex, in a small cottage built in the grounds of a large house. She was employed by the architect who had designed the house to oversee the design of the gardens and she found herself working with several under-gardeners who looked after the plants and trees on the property. The Brights went to visit her every summer, taking the train, which was a lovely treat for everyone. Sam was fond of engines and for days before they travelled he would go round the house, chuffing and puffing away to himself, pretending to be a steam locomotive.

Aunt Lizzie could do everything, Cecily often thought. She'd made clothes for the dolls, just as Papa had promised, even if there were not enough of these to fill the wardrobe. Cecily wrote to her aunt every week, telling her the news from Chelsea and Aunt Lizzie always answered by return of post.

Cecily liked playing with the da Pontes because she was able to make their lives happy. Above all, she could see to it that no one in her doll's house ever died. Dying, she decided, was simply not allowed. Mama da Ponte was kind and pretty and did all the things that Cecily's mama used to do.

Cecily shivered and pulled her coat more closely round her. How cold it was! Sam didn't seem to notice it, probably because he'd run on ahead of her.

"Come here, Sam," she called out. "We must start looking for poor little Mossy."

CHAPTER THREE

Meeting the Templetons

The two children had knocked on three front doors and asked three different housemaids about Mossy, but no one had seen her. Everybody they met was very kind and promised to look out for her, but Cecily was beginning to wonder whether they'd ever be reunited with their kitten again and she could feel sadness beginning to weigh her down, as though someone had draped a heavy blanket over her shoulders.

Sam was pulling at her skirt. "Look, Cecily," he said suddenly. "Look there! It's that man!"

"Which man? Where?"

"Just beyond the lamp post. There!"

Cecily peered into the mist, which had crept up from the river and was now making it hard to see clearly. "It's Mr. Templeton," she said.

Sam was too young to know his name but he recognized him, of course. Everyone in the street knew Roderick Templeton by sight, and anyone older than Sam also knew who he was. According to Amy (who had the details from Jemima, the Chistlehursts' parlourmaid), Mr. Templeton was a very well-known person indeed. He was a painter who specialized in portraits of society ladies, and scenes of town life which showed poor orphans seeking shelter from storms and being comforted by kind benefactors. This part of Chelsea was quite famous for being a home to painters, according to Jemima. There was Mr. James Whistler, for instance, who was an American and also spent a great deal of time in Paris, but nevertheless liked painting pictures of London and lived very close by indeed. Amy and Cecily had seen one of Mr. Templeton's paintings reproduced in a magazine belonging to Amy's father. This was, rather unusually, a picture of a woodland scene and there were some deer in the foreground.

Mr. Templeton was a red-faced man with fuzzy grey mutton-chop whiskers and a loud voice. He always wore a long, dark green cloak over his clothes and a tall hat and because he was a big man, you could see him coming from a long way off and sometimes hear him as well, as he was given to singing snatches of songs from the latest Gilbert and Sullivan operetta. The famous painter lived with his daughter, who was tall and slender and could often be seen striding out in the direction of the river.

Mr. Templeton was approaching his gate. Cecily was just wondering whether she dared go up to him and ask him about Mossy, when he raised his voice and called out to her and Sam.

"I say! Children! Come here, please. There's nothing to be afraid of!"

Cecily looked round. There were no other children to be seen anywhere. He was talking to them. She took a deep breath and said, "If you please, sir, we're looking for our kitten."

"Aha! I knew it! I knew that two young 'uns wandering like ghosts in the mist could only be searching for something very precious...for example, a kitten."

"Have you seen Mossy?" Sam asked. "She's black and white. She's very small."

"Well, bless my soul, I think I have. I think your search may be over. Just such a creature ran into my house not two hours ago. My daughter has found a basket for the little thing, I believe, and is feeding her with the very best milk a cow has to offer. Come in, come in, and you may take your pet home."

"Thank you, sir!" Cecily was filled with relief. "It's very kind of you to look after Mossy."

"Not at all…and you've saved me the trouble of knocking at every house in the street. This calls for a celebratory cup of something…warm milk, I daresay, for this young man. And perhaps a cup of tea for a grown-up young lady such as yourself."

Mr. Templeton stood aside and gestured to Cecily and Sam to go up the steps to the front door ahead of him. Cecily felt as though she were one of the society ladies Amy had described, on her way to have her portrait painted. One thing was certain: it was impossible to feel nervous or frightened while you were talking to Mr. Templeton. He was a very comforting sort of gentleman.

Cecily was making a mental note of how she would describe Miss Templeton to Amy. Very slender. Tall and with hair so dark and glossy that it shone in the lamplight. At first, she'd not thought her hostess very pretty, but the more she looked, the more she liked Miss Templeton's face. I shall tell Amy she's beautiful,

Cecily decided. I think she is. Her skin is very pale and her eyes are blue. She knew that those words couldn't possibly describe what she was truly like. If only Amy could meet this new acquaintance! Miss Templeton was quite plainly dressed in a brown skirt and a white blouse, with a cameo brooch at the neck, but she'd wrapped herself in a shawl which was the colour of the sea: between blue and green and with long fringes on it that moved like fronds of seaweed when she raised her arms.

They were sitting in the front parlour of the house. Cecily was waiting for the cup of tea on the small table beside her to cool down. Sam was on the floor, near the fire, stroking Mossy, who had curled up in the basket Miss Templeton had found for her, blissfully asleep and snoring a little. The parlourmaid who'd brought in the tea had also taken some toy soldiers and a kaleidoscope out of a corner cupboard and put them on the hearthrug ready for Sam to play with.

The parlour was so full of furniture and ornaments that it seemed more like a shop than a room in someone's house. You could scarcely see the wallpaper for pictures: portraits, landscapes, watercolours, oils, drawings, all of which, Cecily supposed, must be Mr. Templeton's work. She knew that however hard she tried, she'd never be able to remember everything that was in them. I'll tell Amy, she thought, that they were highly-coloured and full of interesting objects and people.

"You're admiring my father's work," Miss Templeton said.

"It's very…" Cecily couldn't think of an appropriate word. She glanced at the mantelpiece, where she could see several photographs in silver frames, grouped around a clock. The photographs were of pretty girls wearing blouses with lacy collars. They had ribbons in their hair and were gazing at the world with soulful looks on their faces.

"I like those," she said, pointing. "They're like real people who're alive and might speak at any moment."

Just then, Mr. Templeton came into the room and

Miss Templeton said, "Why, Papa...this young lady has praised my portraits of Gertie and Maud. She has great good taste, has she not?"

"Nonsense, dear," said Mr. Templeton. "She is – and no offence is intended, young lady, for you cannot help your age – an unsophisticated child. She cannot be expected to appreciate Art at her age. Although it has to be said that with her hair and her height she would have been an excellent model for Mr. Millais, for instance. How would you have liked to lie in a bath and pose for a portrait of Ophelia like Miss Lizzie Siddall? Not a bit comfortable, I shouldn't think. But at least done in the cause of Art. One needs a certain training, a certain experience to appreciate painting. There are those who claim...my daughter is one of them...that Mr. Whistler, and even more than him, these Impressionists, as they call themselves...are the coming thing, but I believe in the classical virtues. An *impression* is all very well, but not what one requires from a painting, I feel. There needs to be great skill in imitating nature. And that skill is often only appreciated after much study. One can see all that's in a mere photograph, on the other hand, straight away. It's something that requires neither experience nor great delicacy of understanding."

He sat down and beamed at Cecily. Miss Templeton said, "My dearest papa is the best father in the world, but he is old-fashioned. And not a great admirer of Mr. Whistler and the others. As for photography, it's the art of the future. He's frightened that, very soon, Lady This and the Duchess of That will be summoning me and not him to make portraits of them and his nose will be thoroughly out of joint."

"Rosalind is a stout fighter in the cause of her craft." Mr. Templeton smiled and took a sip from his teacup. "But *craft*, not art, is what it is and the enthusiasm will pass, I'm sure of it." He turned to his daughter. "You will marry, my dear, and this foolishness, this traipsing hither and yon carrying baskets of heavy equipment will be forgotten."

"I may marry, Papa," Miss Templeton said, and Cecily noticed that in spite of her calm tone, she was frowning and trying not to sound irritated. "But married or not, I will continue to photograph the world as I see it."

"But why should that be necessary?" Mr. Templeton nearly jumped out of his chair. "The world is all around us. Any one of us may see it and wonder. It takes a painter's art to transform it into something... something more than the ordinary. More than simply what we *see*. And besides," he announced as though he were a conjuror drawing a rabbit out of a top hat, "all your photographs are black and white and shades of grey and sometimes that brownish colour you dignify with the name of 'sepia' but that is not what we see with our eyes. We see an entire spectrum of colour... You cannot match a painter for colour. Try to deny it."

Cecily opened her mouth to say something and then closed it again. Mr. Templeton was right about the colour, but nevertheless... Miss Templeton noticed her and said, "My dear, you want to say something…what is it?"

"I was only going to say that those young ladies will never be seen quite like this again and when they're old this will remind them of how they were…*exactly* how they were…on this one day. When they were young."

Miss Templeton jumped up from the sofa and ran to where Cecily was sitting and took her hand. "You are a very clever girl…you see exactly what I've been trying to tell my father for years. The moment…*that moment*…lives for ever. That's it! Exactly."

"Why is my painting not capturing a moment in the same way? Eh? Answer me that, if you can!"

"Because we have no assurance that you haven't tinkered with the reality of the scene before you, for some reason of your own. Some artistic reason." Miss Templeton smiled. "Why, you might decide to change the colour of a flower so as to make a harmony with someone's dress. You might make it quite different from what it is in real life."

"Real life," said Mr. Templeton, "is not the point. Beauty is the point." He said this with an air of someone who wasn't going to discuss the matter any further and indeed, he turned to Cecily at once and said, "I'm sorry, my dear. We've been so busy revisiting our old battlefields that we've been most remiss about asking your names."

"I'm Cecily Bright," said Cecily. "My brother's name is Samuel. We call him Sam."

"How delightful!" Mr. Templeton beamed. "I was at the theatre last night, at the first night of Mr. Oscar Wilde's new play, which is called *The Importance of Being Earnest*. I'm quite sure you've heard of Mr. Wilde…in my opinion, quite the wittiest man in London. And an admirer, I may say, of my work. And in last night's play, one of the heroines was called *Cecily*, just like you! A remarkable coincidence, I call that!"

"Papa," Miss Templeton said, "I think the children should be getting along now. It's almost dark outside and their parents will be wondering where they are."

She turned to Cecily. "I'll take you home directly, but first would you like to visit my studio?"

"Oh, yes, I would love to! Thank you!"

"We must be quite quick then…"

Cecily jumped up from her chair. The clock on the mantelpiece stood at half past four. "I forgot about the time." She didn't say *because I was enjoying myself so much*, but that was what she meant. "But I would love to see your studio."

"A lot of boxes on stilts up there…strange machines with lenses that you look through and which show you the image upside down! Newfangled nonsense!" This was Mr. Templeton, who had moved to the hearthrug to play soldiers with Sam.

Miss Templeton laughed. "Take no notice, Cecily. Follow me to the second floor. Rather a lot of stairs, I'm afraid, but the light up there is just what I require."

CHAPTER FOUR

A Room Full of Magic

The room that Miss Templeton called her studio took up most of the second floor. It had two enormous windows whose curtains hadn't yet been drawn. Cecily could see a wide expanse of violet sky, and the occasional snowflake drifted across the glass. The room was full of so many interesting things that Cecily could scarcely take them in at once. There were cameras, of course: two of them, one smaller than the other. Miss Templeton said, "That's the one I take about with me when I go outdoors. It's lighter than the big one and takes photographs just as well." Each camera was a brown wooden box, with a concertina-like part on the front of it ("the bellows" Miss Templeton said that was called), and bound about with very shiny brass fittings. Cecily could see a tripod, like a set of skinny wooden legs, with a black cloth draped over it.

"I have to cover my head when I'm composing a photograph," Miss Templeton explained, "and when I look through the lens I see my subject upside down, but of course it all comes out the right way up when the photograph is developed. Then, when I'm sure I have the precise image I want, I come out and stand beside the tripod to take the picture. After that, the glass plate needs to be developed in the dark room. That's in the basement, and it's where I keep my chemicals, too, because Papa hates the smells. How dark or bright the photograph appears depends on the amount of light I allow in through the lens. *Photography* means 'drawing with light'…did you know that? It's from the Greek. I have to dip my photographic plates into all sorts of strange substances to make the picture appear and then soak them in a fixer, which means I can keep the image for ever."

"I'd love to see how the photographs are made," Cecily said. Suddenly, she longed to know all about the magical process that could result in pictures that were so lifelike.

"I'll show you another day, Cecily. I'll explain the magic, I promise."

Was Miss Templeton inviting her to visit again? How wonderful! Next time, Cecily resolved, she would bring Amy with her. She looked round the studio, while Miss Templeton picked up various items and tidied them away into an enormous chest of drawers. "I'm very organized when it comes to my work," she said, "but somehow my studio becomes untidy, in spite of my best efforts."

Leaning against one wall was a huge pain

garden. It was almost the same height and wic

the room itself, and it showed arches with roses growing over them, and a lot of trees and grass in the middle distance and a great deal of blue sky dotted with fluffy white clouds. Set in front of the painting was a bench, and also an urn, and a wickerwork chair next to a small table covered with a white cloth.

"Ah yes," said Miss Templeton. "I use that as a backdrop. My father painted it for me, which is kind of him, considering how set he is against photography. There are a great many scenes which I can photograph against that background. For instance, come and sit down for a moment…"

Cecily sat down on the wicker chair, as instructed.

"Now…I had a pretty straw hat somewhere…" Miss Templeton went over to a cupboard on the other side of the room and opened it. Cecily could see from where she was sitting that it was overflowing with gloves, shoes, scarves and hatboxes. Some garments were hanging up, just as though this were a normal cupboard in an ordinary house.

"Perfect..." Miss Templeton was pushing back Cecily's hair and she felt she had to say something.

"I'm sorry my hair's so unruly. Nanny Mildred calls it that."

"It's most beautiful...why, half the paintings Papa and his friends admire...the Pre-Raphaelite brotherhood...have ladies in them with hair like yours. Now tuck this rose under the ribbon...there...and we can pretend that you're Mr. Wilde's Cecily."

Miss Templeton picked up a looking glass from the top of the chest of drawers so that Cecily could see herself transformed. Then she put it down again next to an untidy heap of jewellery: necklaces, brooches, rings and a tiara.

"You're rather tall for Cecily," Miss Templeton said, "and perhaps rather too slender. You'd be a better Gwendolen, I think. I could dress you very smartly. Gwendolen's a very elegant London lady down in the country for the day. If only we had someone to be a pretty country girl, I would compose a scene from *The Importance of Being Earnest*. Cecily in the play turns out to be much cleverer than everyone thinks, of course. It's quite delightful."

"My friend Amy is pretty and dainty," said Cecily, feeling her heart beat a little faster.

"You must bring her here to meet me," said Miss Templeton.

"Oh, I will. She'd love that, I know. Thank you! May we come and see you after school tomorrow?"

"Certainly. That would be excellent. I can think of several poses I might photograph you in. Perhaps some scenes from Shakespeare...or a fairy tale."

She came over to Cecily and took off the hat. "I must walk you back to your house now, my dear, or your parents will think you've been stolen away."

"My papa will not be back from work yet, and my mama is dead."

Cecily blushed. Why had she said that?

"Poor child." Miss Templeton put an arm around Cecily's shoulders. "I'm so, so sorry. Let us go and find your brother. And little Mossy, too."

The three of them, Cecily, Sam and Miss Templeton, made their way back to Number Six in the dark. Miss Templeton was carrying a cat basket. She'd shown Sam where the holes were that would allow Mossy to breathe, because he'd looked very worried to see his kitten shut up in such a small space. When they arrived at the steps that led up to their own front door, Sam ran ahead and lifted the knocker and let it drop.

Florrie answered the door. "Master Sam!" she said. "Thank goodness you're home safe. Nanny and I were about to come and look for you." She took the basket from Miss Templeton. "Thank you, Miss, for bringing the children home."

"We found Mossy!" Sam ran inside, and Florrie followed him. Cecily turned to say goodbye.

"Thank you very much, Miss Templeton."

"Rosalind," said Miss Templeton. "The other's such a mouthful. And we're friends, are we not?"

"Oh, yes!" said Cecily. "And I'll bring Amy to meet you tomorrow."

She watched Miss Templeton walking away into the night. *Rosalind.* A beautiful name for a beautiful person. She couldn't wait to tell Amy all about her.

"Cecily, my dear," said John Bright, "you may come into the drawing room after Sam is in bed, and say good evening to my guests."

Cecily looked up from her bread-and-butter pudding. Papa had come into the nursery, as he often did when he returned from work, to talk to her and Sam before bedtime.

"Thank you, Papa…" She was about to tell her father about Mossy's disappearance and their search and how it ended, but Sam began to babble about it in his headlong way so she fell silent. Papa smiled as he listened and looked at Cecily over Sam's head as he gave his son a hug. "I'm sure you'll tell me this story in a more measured way, won't you?"

"Yes, Papa. I will, I promise. Who has come to visit?"

"Mr. Collins, Mr. Drayton and Miss Braithwaite. I daresay we shall play a rubber of bridge when you've gone up to bed."

He stood up. "Goodnight, Sam…" He kissed the top of Sam's head and left the room.

"Come on, Sam," Cecily said. "*Up the wooden stairs to Bedfordshire…*"

Sam laughed. That was what Florrie always said and he found it funny. Cecily was happy to see him in such good spirits. She read to Sam every night from his book of nursery rhymes or thought of a story to tell him. He liked adventures with pirates in them and Cecily had no difficulty in inventing tales that he enjoyed. Tonight, she would try to think of a story about Mossy.

CHAPTER FIVE

The Poor da Pontes!

Cecily sat at the table in the nursery, writing a letter to Aunt Lizzie. She sucked the end of her pen and turned the paper over to write a second page.

...and at first we felt a little shy, but Rosalind insisted that she did not wish to be called "Miss Templeton" because that made her seem like one of our teachers, when really she thinks of us as friends. I wish you could meet her, Aunt Lizzie, for she is so interesting and charming.

She is employed in a studio in the West End, as an assistant to a gentleman who takes photographs of families and children and anyone who requires a portrait. Rosalind says that it's very fashionable now, having your portrait made in a studio. Mr. Templeton says that however fashionable it becomes, there will never be an end to painted portraiture, but Rosalind thinks he says this to raise his own spirits, because fewer people than before are asking him to paint their wives and children.

Cecily sat back, remembering occasions when the atmosphere in the Templeton house became a little heated as Rosalind and her father argued about art and photography. They always ended such disputes with laughter and friendship, but Cecily had noticed how critical Mr. Templeton was of his daughter's efforts and how harshly he sometimes criticized them. Aunt Lizzie would find it all fascinating, she knew. Cecily started writing again.

Everyone wants wedding photographs and christening photographs and love tokens. Rosalind says it's because they wish to preserve happy memories. She says she'll have a studio of her own one day. I wish I could be her assistant, though I haven't told her this. We have now visited her several times since Mossy ran away, and I've watched her composing tableaux: dressing and posing her subjects, and one day I will learn about the darkroom work as well. I've discovered that Rosalind, too, has no mama. Amy's mother told Amy that Mrs. Templeton left the family when her daughter was very young. She went to Germany with a gentleman who was teaching her to play the piano. There was a scandal at the time, Mrs. Chistlehurst says. I wonder whether Rosalind still misses her mama as much as I do mine.

Cecily and Amy were walking home after another visit to the Templetons' house.

"Do you think," Cecily asked, "that Rosalind really means it? When she says she's always happy to see us? Do you think she'd be relieved if we didn't call on her so often?"

Amy stopped walking and turned to face her friend. "Nonsense, Cecily. You are so timid, truly. Rosalind would not invite us to call and give us tea and let us dress up in her jewels and hats if she didn't want us there. I think she looks on our visits as a relief after her work is done."

"Perhaps she'd like to rest a little? Instead of which, there we are, talking to her and getting under her feet."

"If you're so worried about it, why don't you ask her next time? Then you'll know."

Amy quickened her pace, to show Cecily that she was irritated by her remarks. Cecily followed her friend, resolving to do as she suggested. Amy thinks I won't, she thought. She thinks I'm too shy, but I'm not.

Cecily had suddenly realized that morning, looking at the doll's house in the nursery, that it had been days and days since she and Amy had played with the da Pontes. There was a layer of dust on the miniature furniture and Cecily took the time, before she left the room, to polish the table and the sideboard with a pocket handkerchief. Bambina hadn't been taken out of her cradle for a long time and Paolo and Maggie were lying across the beds as though she'd thrown them there and forgotten about them. Hastily, she'd propped them up at the table and promised herself to play with them as soon as possible.

This neglect was the fault of the photographs. Rosalind had shown them pictures of pretty girls and delightful scenes and though Amy liked these very much, it was Cecily who was particularly enchanted. Amy enjoyed being dressed up as a fairy or a sea nymph, and so did Cecily, but she found herself even more intrigued by the idea of being the person who took the photographs. No one, not even Amy, knew of the secret dream, which she went through every night in bed, before falling asleep. In this fantasy, Rosalind had a studio…in Chelsea, not the West End, for that would mean Cecily wouldn't have to travel so far every day…and all the ladies in the neighbourhood flocked to this place to have portraits made of their babies. These little bundles of lace and frills and delicately-knitted blankets would have to be looked after before and after being posed with their proud parents and that would be Cecily's job at first. Then, when she proved herself to be a reliable nursemaid for the infants, she would be allowed to help with other things: ladies and gentlemen posing for engagement pictures; dramatic tableaux of all kinds; wedding photographs…and in the end, Rosalind would turn to her and say: "Oh, I'm a little fatigued this afternoon, Cecily…I shall leave the day's appointments in your hands."

Cecily could hardly see for tears. She couldn't remember when she'd been so upset. She stood up, ran out of the nursery and flew downstairs. Papa was in the hall, saying goodbye to Ellen Braithwaite and a friend called Roland, who had been visiting again, as they did so often.

"Cecily!" Papa said. "Whatever is the matter?"

"It's the da Pontes, Papa… Sam. It must be Sam. And Mossy…he's let Mossy into the nursery even though I've told him over and over again she must be kept away from my doll's house…"

"Excuse me, please, Ellen…Roland," Papa said. Then he drew Cecily aside and said, "Go to the nursery, my dear. I will say goodbye to our guests and come up at once. I promise. Dry your tears and wait for me."

Cecily sniffed and muttered something inaudible and made her way upstairs again. She opened the nursery door, and sat down at the table, trying hard not to look at the doll's house.

It's my fault, she thought, as she waited for her father to come up. My fault for not taking proper care of the da Pontes for such a long time. I should have made sure the door was properly closed. Sam didn't mean any harm, but where was Nanny? Downstairs talking to Cook, probably. Surely six years old was grown up enough to know that if a kitten who was well-known for her friskiness begins to play with dolls, you were supposed to pick her up and remove her from the scene? Cecily was suddenly furious with her little brother…oh, if only he wasn't in bed, how she would scold him! Poor Mossy probably thought that the da Pontes were an unusual breed of mouse!

"Now," said Papa, coming in and going straight over to the doll's house. "What's happened here?"

"Sam…he and Mossy have been playing in here. Nanny's told him over and over again but he won't listen."

"He's very young, Cecily." Papa had kneeled down beside the house and, picking up the dolls one by one, he placed them on the table in front of Cecily and she burst into tears all over again.

"Look at them, Papa!" Mossy had shredded Mama da Ponte's dress; poor little Paolo's foot had been chewed nearly through and Bambina had been taken out of her cradle and dragged about so violently that her head was almost severed from her body.

"Nothing we cannot mend, Cecily," Papa said, turning the dolls over carefully. He took his daughter's hand across the table. "Do you remember how we finished making the house together? How we looked forward to sticking the wallpaper to the walls? What I remember is how you helped me, Cecily. I couldn't have done it alone, you know. It was such a sad time, was it not?"

Cecily looked up and saw that her father's eyes were bright with tears. She had never seen him crying properly, in the way that she and Sam often cried…of course not. Gentlemen did not weep in that fashion, but his eyes had often been red-rimmed and she could see by the set of his mouth and the stiffness in his body that he was unhappy. Now, the tears were almost there, on his cheeks. She said quickly, "I do remember, Papa. And I know the dolls can be mended, but it was… a shock. And I'm angry with Sam, too. He's in bed, and I can't tell him how angry I am."

"Don't be too hard on him, Cecily. He's young, as I

said. But he probably feels upset about it, too. He may have hidden away in his bed to avoid your anger…"

"I won't shout at him. I'll just tell him to be more careful. May I do that?"

Papa nodded and stood up. "You, too, should be in bed, I'm sure."

"May I ask you something, Papa?" Cecily spoke before she'd properly thought about it and now that she had, she was nervous about speaking, but there was nothing to be done.

"Certainly, my dear."

"Do you like Miss Braithwaite?"

"What a strange question! Certainly I like her. She is pleasant and kind and we have many things in common. She's a good friend. Why do you ask such a thing?"

"I wondered, that's all," said Cecily. "Goodnight, Papa."

"Goodnight." Papa kissed the top of her head and left the room.

Cecily thought about what her father had said. Pleasant and kind…did that indicate love? She didn't think so, but intended to ask Amy's opinion again. What was certainly true was that Miss Braithwaite was a frequent visitor to Number Six, Chelsea Walk.

CHAPTER SIX

A Surprise for Cecily

Cecily was writing an account for Aunt Lizzie of what had happened to her dolls.

...I fear you may have to make a new dress for Mama da Ponte. Florrie did a bit of stitching and she's done her best but she is not as good at sewing as you are and it looks mended and patched and horrid. Do you have any pretty material for such a thing? I hope so.

We're already talking about when you next come to see

us. I wish it could be before your birthday, but Papa says the time will fly. I don't think it ever does if you're really waiting for something. It only goes by quickly while you're enjoying yourself. Sam is being especially good whenever he sees me today because he knows that letting Mossy get at the doll's house was his fault. He is keeping to his room a great deal and being much quieter than usual.

"Cecily! Come here, Cecily!"

That was Sam calling her. Cecily sighed. What was the matter with him now? She'd forgiven him for allowing Mossy to wreak havoc in the doll's house and he'd been good for some days. Today was Sunday. The Brights had just come back from church, and Cecily had been reading the Lambs' *Tales From Shakespeare*. After lunch, she would write again to Aunt Lizzie about Rosalind's plan to photograph her and Amy as characters from Mr. Shakespeare's plays. At school, she and Amy had enjoyed studying *A Midsummer Night's Dream* and *The Merchant of*

Venice and she'd been consulting Lamb to see what other heroines there were to choose from.

"Quick, Cecily!"

Sam didn't sound in any distress. Rather, he was excited. She ran up the stairs to the second floor and there he was, in the doorway of the back bedroom. Behind him, she could see the furniture shrouded in white sheets.

"Nanny Mildred will scold you for playing up here, Sam. What are you doing?"

"She said I could come. Florrie saw a mouse."

"In here? How could she? The door's always kept shut."

"On the landing. It was there she saw it. It ran under the door. Nanny said to bring Mossy up to hunt the mouse."

"And has she found it?"

"No, but she's in the corner. Maybe the mouse hole's there."

"Why do you need me, Sam? I was busy."

"I wanted you to see…" His voice faded away.

Cecily went in. Mossy was indeed crouched by the far wall, just near the corner, trying to look like a fearsome predator. The skirting board didn't quite meet the floorboards in some places. A mouse could easily have run into one of the gaps in the panelling.

"That's the mouse hole," Sam said.

"How d'you know? Did you see anything run in there?"

"No, but a mouse could fit." He got down on the floor and stretched out next to Mossy.

"Get up this minute, Sam! Your clothes will be filthy and Nanny will blame me for allowing you to lie around in the dust. Get up! You're not going to see a mouse. Neither is Mossy. Any mouse who knows what's good for him will keep well hidden with a cat sitting outside his front door."

"But I see something. Look…" He put two fingers into the hole and pulled out a small square of cardboard.

"Give that to me," Cecily said, and she put it in her

pocket without looking at it. "And now get up and come downstairs. Mossy'll wait for the mouse, and we'll leave the door open just a little so she can come out when she's found him. Aren't you hungry? It's nearly lunchtime, and I'm going to try and clean you up before Nanny sees you."

The promise of food succeeded in luring Sam out of the room.

Later that afternoon, Cecily went to show the piece of cardboard to her father. He had studied the history of the house and knew about the people who had lived here, long ago. She blushed as she handed it over to him, because the picture on it was of a lady with very few clothes on, and indeed, Papa coughed and looked away a little as he told Cecily what he thought it was.

"Here's the date, do you see? 1764… It's a ticket of admission to Ranelagh Gardens, which in those days was a place of entertainment and amusement, just where the park is now. Most interesting…perhaps one of the young ladies who came to school here long ago went to the Gardens, though it's hard to imagine the teachers letting their charges visit such a place. Ah well, it is a message from the past. Perhaps one day I will take it to a meeting of the Local History Society. Most interesting."

He stood up and went to put the cardboard ticket in a drawer, but Cecily said, "Papa, may I keep it? Sam found it, but I would like to put it in my scrapbook."

Her father hesitated, then gave her the ticket. "I'm not sure whether it's quite suitable...this drawing..."

"It was a ticket, Papa, so it must be respectable, surely."

"The eighteenth century was a much laxer time in many ways..."

"Please, Papa..."

"Will you undertake not to show it to anyone?"

"Amy? May I show it to her?"

Papa would relent. He almost always did, when

Cecily looked both eager and anxious. "Very well." He sighed and went to the door. "But only Amy, please. And I hope I may borrow it if I wish?"

"Yes, of course you may. Thank you, Papa."

Cecily stared down at the yellowing card, with its edges worn away a little. It had stayed there, hidden in the panelling for more than a hundred years and now here it was, like a faint whisper from the past and she wondered who the young girl was who must have known Ranelagh Gardens in 1764. Perhaps her ghost might indeed be a visitor to the room. She shivered pleasurably and looked forward to discussing the likelihood of this with Amy.

The next day, after they had left their school things at home, Cecily and Amy went straight to the Templetons' house and upstairs to the studio. While the girls enjoyed the warm milk and buttered scones that Elsie the parlourmaid had brought in, they listened to Rosalind telling them of her plans for the afternoon's session.

"I've been considering who you girls might be," she said, "and I think Juliet for you, Amy, from *Romeo and Juliet*, of course. Miranda for you, Cecily, from *The Tempest*. Do you know the play?"

Cecily said, "I've read the story in the Lambs' *Tales*."

"Excellent." Rosalind smiled. "Then you know that she and her father have been shipwrecked on an island, and that gives me an opportunity to suggest the sea behind you…there!"

She uncovered a flat painting of the ocean, with rocks sticking out of a stretch of sand in the foreground. "Here's one of Papa's early landscapes and just the thing, I think. Miranda will be wearing fine clothes, but they'll have been torn and tossed about a little in the storm… The effect I seek is: windswept. Your hair streaming down…wild, untamed."

Cecily didn't feel she could say what she thought, which was: why do I have to be wild and untamed, with torn and windswept clothes? Why can't I be one of the well-dressed heroines, like Juliet or Titania?

It would be rude to complain. I'd rather do what Rosalind suggests, she told herself, than not be photographed at all.

"But let's start with you, Amy. Juliet dressed for the ball at the beginning of the play and leaning over the balcony."

Amy beamed and looked pleased with herself. Cecily could see the white dress, hanging up ready for her to put on, and a beautiful headdress and jewels to go with it. Cecily thought it would have been much more interesting to show Juliet stretched out on her tomb. Anyone knows, she said to herself, that the balcony scene needs Romeo in it. The photograph would be incomplete. She stood up and went to find the velvet cloak that Rosalind had decided she must wear over the torn brocade dress that she'd provided for Miranda.

Cecily watched for what seemed like a very long time while Amy's picture was set up and she tried to follow how Rosalind decided what would make the best picture. She disappeared for several minutes under her cloth and looked through the lens, moving the bellows backwards and forwards, which Cecily knew altered the amount of light that came in through the lens. From her bent-over position she called to Amy to move this way and then that. Posed against a flowerpot. Against a door. Leaning over a fragment of a wrought-iron gate that would be most effective, Rosalind said, as a balcony. While she waited, Cecily wondered where the Templetons found the bits and pieces that their house was full of. There were no paintings of the sea nor sections of gate at Number Six. Perhaps that was the difference between artists and ordinary people. When I grow up, she resolved, I will fill my house with unusual items of every sort.

The photograph was taken at last, and Amy said, "May I go home now, Rosalind? I promised my mama to read stories to the little ones tonight… Will you manage on your own, Cecily?"

"Certainly." Cecily tried not to sound too annoyed.

How typical of Amy to think she was the one in charge, the one without whom nothing could happen. Especially since it was Sam and Cecily who were the first to meet the Templetons! "I am able to find my own front door, I think."

But Amy had already left the room and was on her way downstairs.

Cecily didn't often admit it to herself, but without Amy, she enjoyed Rosalind's company even more. They spent happy minutes arranging the cloak to look particularly windswept.

"Did Miranda not have a mother?" Cecily asked.

"No, she was like you and me… Your poor mama died when you were six, I believe. That must have been terrible."

"How did you know I was six?"

"Amy said something…" Cecily knew that Amy had spoken about her and she felt a little irritated.

"I have no mama either," Rosalind said, "but I was a great deal older when mine left us. She lives abroad.

Papa and I have had to fend for ourselves for many years. Now, stand up straight as though you were looking out to sea."

The subject, Cecily could see, was one that Rosalind didn't wish to speak about. She disappeared behind the camera and was lost under the black cloth till she took the photograph. When they had finished, Cecily began to help with the task of putting the props and costumes away, but just then, there came a knocking at the door. It was Elsie again.

"Elsie, you can see that I'm busy…" Rosalind began.

"I think you should come downstairs, Miss Rosalind," Elsie said. "Mr. John Bright has called for his daughter. I've asked him to wait in the parlour."

CHAPTER SEVEN

Papa is Displeased

"Good afternoon, Mr. Bright," said Rosalind. "I'm sorry to keep you waiting. My name is Rosalind Templeton. I've been photographing Cecily and her friend Amy, too, for a series of pictures I'm composing, based on Shakespeare's heroines."

Cecily was relieved that she was no longer dressed in her costume. She could see that Papa was upset. He'd be polite, she knew, because he'd never met

Rosalind, but she feared that his displeasure might later be directed at her. He said, "Good afternoon, Miss Templeton. I've been concerned about Cecily, not knowing where she was. She is out very late. I was obliged to call on the Chistlehursts. Amy informed me of my daughter's whereabouts."

"I am so sorry," Rosalind said. "We lose ourselves in the work, and then forget to look at the clock. This is entirely my fault."

"I feel that Cecily, too, bears some of the blame. She knows when she has to come home. She has her schoolwork to complete every day, of course."

"Of course. I hope you'll allow the girls to visit me again. They are such good subjects."

"I cannot speak for Amy Chistlehurst, naturally, but Cecily will in future ask my permission whenever she wishes to visit you."

It seemed to Cecily that this meant seeing a great deal less of Rosalind. If Papa allowed her to come, it would certainly not be every day, nor probably, every week. He would think that visiting so often was impolite. He might even try to stop her coming at all. Perhaps he thought an artist's house was not the sort of place he'd want his daughter to visit.

Papa had calmed down somewhat, Cecily saw, though she feared he was still angry with her. He said, "Thank you, Miss Templeton. Now, Cecily, gather your things together and we will return home."

As soon as they reached Number Six, Papa called Cecily into his study.

"What have you to say for yourself, Cecily?" he asked, looking stern.

"I am very sorry to have made you worry, Papa. I should have been home earlier but forgot the time."

Papa frowned. "I want you to spend more time under this roof and less under the Templetons'. I had a word with Nanny before setting out to find you today and she tells me that you've been visiting almost daily. That must stop."

"But, Papa, did you not like Miss Templeton? Mr. Templeton is a well-known painter. And have you seen the photographs? They are so wonderful!"

"Miss Templeton seemed agreeable. And I did look at the photographs, while I was waiting for you to come down from the studio."

"Did you not think them fine? Do you not see how lifelike and clear they are? Just as though you were in front of the real person. The camera performs magic."

"I'm the first to agree that the camera is a great step forward in scientific invention and no doubt will have many uses in the future. And Miss Templeton's images are admirable, but that has nothing to do with what I'm saying. Nothing at all. You simply cannot dress yourself up in ridiculous costumes and pose for pictures every afternoon."

"It's not every afternoon that we pose. Indeed, before today, it's been some time since Rosalind took our picture."

"*Rosalind?* She allows you to call her by her Christian name?"

Cecily nodded. "Is that wrong of her, do you think?"

"Perhaps not wrong exactly, but still, it strikes me as a little…Bohemian, perhaps. How many other ladies do you call by their given names? Do you call Miss Braithwaite *Ellen*?"

Cecily shook her head. She couldn't imagine calling Miss Braithwaite anything more personal than *Miss Braithwaite*, however long she knew her.

"Well, then," said Papa. "Do we have an agreement, Cecily? You will not visit without my express permission?"

Cecily nodded and wondered what she could possibly do to change Papa's mind. She resolved to discuss it with Amy at school next day.

Cecily and Amy sat at the back of the room during Needlework Hour. The pale, April sunshine fell on their backs as they talked quietly together. Miss Perry, their teacher, suffered from a slight deafness, which meant her classroom was always filled with the sound of girls whispering to one another while someone's French knots and slip stitches were receiving Miss Perry's full attention.

"Don't worry," Amy said. "He will relent in time. Next time you ask him, he's sure to say you may visit."

"I hope you're right. Today I went to see him again and he said maybe in a little while."

"Well, then…" Amy bent her head to the leaf she was embroidering on to a traycloth. Her needlework was a little slapdash, Cecily thought and took pleasure in comparing Amy's stitches with her own far neater ones. There weren't many subjects in which she felt confident that her work was as good as her friend's. Amy doesn't mind not visiting the Templetons, Cecily thought. She'd happily forget about Rosalind and the studio and the photographs if it weren't for me. She has her brothers and sisters to think of, and much else to do. Also, she doesn't want to be a photographer when she grows up. She's not like me.

"I think," Amy said, "that you must give him a reason to visit the studio."

"What sort of reason?"

"Well, would he not want his own photograph taken, perhaps?"

"Whatever for?"

"I don't know. To mark some occasion: an engagement, a wedding, a birth."

How tactless of Amy, Cecily thought, to mention engagements and weddings when she knows how much I worry about Miss Braithwaite! But an idea came to Cecily then. She was so happy to have thought of it, so excited to imagine how it might be achieved, that she pricked her finger and had to suck it quickly to prevent a drop of blood from falling on her traycloth.

"It's Aunt Lizzie's birthday next month... I will ask Papa if we might make a family portrait...him and me and Sam and even Mossy...to give her as a gift... Oh, surely, *surely* he'll see that's an excellent notion! She's always been interested in modern inventions, and a woman photographer is something she would heartily approve of. I can't think of anything that would give her more pleasure."

"Wouldn't she prefer a beautiful hat? A pair of white leather gloves, trimmed with beading? A necklace? A ticket to the Savoy Theatre?"

"Oh, Amy, you don't know Aunt Lizzie as I do! She is not a white leather gloves kind of person. I promise you, she would treasure a photograph of us." Cecily leaned forward and whispered in Amy's ear. "I fear she had a tragic love affair when she was younger and will never marry now…and never have children. She would have wished to be a mother, I'm sure. And Sam and I are the nearest thing she has to a son and daughter of her own."

"Well, you know your own aunt best, I suppose," said Amy. "Why don't you ask your papa and see what he says?"

For a moment, Cecily imagined Papa laughing at her idea and being almost as scornful as Amy, but she pushed this thought away and turned to her embroidery again, concentrating instead on a dream of herself, Sam, and Papa with Mossy in a basket, walking along the street towards the Templetons' house.

CHAPTER EIGHT

The Bright Family Portrait

Cecily was telling Aunt Lizzie in a letter how much she missed being able to visit the Templeton house as often as she used to.

Papa should realize, she wrote, *that we learned so much from Rosalind…more than we do in our classes at school. She showed us photographs in periodicals and told us all about the actors and actresses shown in them, performing in Shakespeare's plays. We talked about the clothes that the society ladies wear in the illlustrated papers. We saw pictures of the Queen, too, in a black dress with a lace collar. And I know a lot about the painters Mr. Templeton admires and the ones he does not. He is very rude about someone called James McNeill Whistler and about Mr. Turner, who lives very near to Chelsea Walk, but Rosalind admires these gentlemen greatly. She likes French painters best of all, like Monsieur Cézanne and Monsieur Monet and Monsieur Degas. Mr. Templeton sniffed loudly whenever Rosalind mentioned their names. He called them Impressionists and made it sound like something no one would ever want to be.*

Cecily looked at her father, who was sitting on the end of her bed. She leaned back against the pillows. "You said you'd think about it, Papa. What I suggested for Aunt Lizzie's birthday present. Have you thought?"

"I have, Cecily, and I must say, I am not entirely convinced it's a good idea. Would Lizzie truly like such a thing? Or are you simply trying to persuade me to let you visit Miss Templeton's house again?"

"I *do* want to go back, it's true. You've only given me permission to see her three times since…well, since the day you found me there."

"I don't mean to be unkind, Cecily, but truly, I think you could find more worthwhile activities than dressing up as something or other…what was it last time?"

"Cinderella," Cecily answered. "What's wrong with that?"

She thought back to how they had laughed together, she and Rosalind, while they were arranging and adjusting the rags suitable to the part.

"Do you want to be a clothes horse?" Papa asked. "A model? It seems a singularly limited ambition."

"No, I should like to be the one taking the photographs. I'm learning from Miss Templeton all the time. Ladies can work in photographic studios. Miss Templeton herself does. And more and more people, Papa, go and have their photographs taken."

"I cannot imagine why."

"Yes, you can, Papa. Think how a photograph reminds you of someone when they're not there, with you." She hesitated, wondering whether she dared to mention the daguerreotype of her parents in the parlour. Nothing ventured, nothing gained, she told herself. "For instance..." She hesitated.

"Yes? What did you want to say?"

"I still go and look at Mama's picture every day. It's the only thing that can remind me of how she used to be. Without that portrait, I'd have lost her face for ever. Think how dreadful that would be."

Papa stood up and went to kiss Cecily goodnight. "That's quite true. Dear child, you are right. I, too, look at that picture every single day and it *does* bring her back in some small measure."

"Imagine if we had a whole album of photographs of Mama...just as she was. Fixed for ever."

"I see her sometimes in my dreams, as clear as clear." Papa was silent for a few moments and Cecily could see that he was thinking carefully about what she'd said. Finally he smiled at her and said, "One *does* forget…and one should not, if that can be helped. You tell your Miss Templeton that we would like to be photographed as a family. I'm willing to pay the proper rate for the sittings, of course. And you're right. Lizzie *will* be enchanted with such a thing as a birthday present and I, too, will be glad of a memento of your childhood, yours and Sam's, when I'm an old man and you're both quite grown up. Not to mention a picture of myself in my prime which I can look at when I am grey and infirm and confined to a basket chair with a rug over my knees. Goodnight, my dear. Sleep well."

After her father left the room, Cecily noticed that moonlight was coming through the gap in the curtains and filling the room with a silvery light. She got out of bed and went to the window. Looking up, she saw that the moon was almost at the full and she smiled. The nursery rhyme "Hey diddle diddle" was one of Sam's favourites, and the part about the cow jumping over the moon was nonsense, of course, but Cecily still liked to imagine another sort of world up there, far off in the dark, dark blue…how many miles away? She would ask Papa, who was bound to know the answer. She drew the curtains properly and went back to bed, pulling the covers up round her shoulders. Tomorrow, she'd be able to visit Rosalind again. How fortunate it was that Papa had changed his mind.

"It would be more suitable, I think," Rosalind said, "if I were to come to your house. With family portraits, it's always better to place subjects in a setting they know and feel comfortable in. Not everyone is as willing to pose as you and Amy, you know."

Cecily felt happier than she'd felt for a very long time. She was sitting in the Templetons' parlour. Mr. Templeton was hidden behind his newspaper. She'd just explained to Rosalind about Aunt Lizzie's birthday and how she would be visiting them for the day on the 18th of May to celebrate.

"If I may call on you on Sunday," Rosalind said, "when your papa is home from his work, then we can discuss which room and what kind of clothes and so forth, and then the following week, I shall bring the camera and all my equipment. Will that suit?"

"I'll ask Papa," Cecily answered.

Mr. Templeton emerged from behind the rustling pages of his newspaper and said, "Your family might consider a portrait...a painted portrait. I would be delighted. Of course, I charge somewhat more than my daughter, but then I have to work much harder and employ far more artistry, to say nothing of skill... craft...call it what you will. All photographers have to do is look and squeeze something and hey presto, the picture is there!"

"Now, Papa, stop that at once! The picture is not immediately there, as you've said. I have to develop the film. It's a long and quite complicated process. Poor Cecily does not wish to be impolite, I'm sure, so I will point out to you some drawbacks in what you propose. Sam, who is only six, won't be able to pose without moving for sitting after sitting. And then there's the cat, Mossy…"

"The one we rescued?"

"The very same. Now much grown, I feel quite sure. Cats, as you know, never do what you want them to."

"Cats are, indeed, altogether unbiddable. Perhaps you're right. I doubt Mossy will even permit herself to be photographed," said Mr. Templeton, and he sighed loudly in mock-distress as he picked up his newspaper again. "Never mind!"

On the day that Rosalind came to call to discuss the photograph of the Bright family, Miss Braithwaite was also visiting, and Cecily wished she was not. She suspected, though she didn't know for certain, that Papa had asked his friend to be there especially, as a kind of protector, because he was a little nervous of Rosalind. This irritated Cecily greatly, and because Amy wasn't there for her to complain to, she fumed inwardly. There were many reasons why she was angry, but the main one was this: Rosalind was almost bound to think that her papa and Miss Braithwaite had an understanding. They did not, she was almost sure of it, though not completely certain. Perhaps, she thought, I should ask him, but what to say? I don't want to put the idea of loving Miss Braithwaite into his head, if it isn't there already. Cecily had seen no real evidence of such feeling, and decided to keep silent on the matter for the moment.

Everyone had gathered in the drawing room, and Miss Braithwaite was pouring the tea that Florrie had just brought in and behaving, Cecily thought, exactly as though she were the mistress of the house. She was wearing a fawn-coloured dress with a paisley-patterned shawl over it and Rosalind sitting beside her looked even prettier than usual. *Her* dress was of a shade between violet and blue and had cuffs trimmed with lace. Her hair was twisted up into a complicated arrangement at the back of her head and held in place by a silver clasp. She had a bag at her feet which contained something rather large and Cecily could see Sam eyeing it with interest.

"We're all very excited," Miss Braithwaite said, "about the proposed photographic session. I was photographed once myself, when I was bridesmaid at a cousin's wedding. One ought to welcome new inventions, I'm sure. It is quite astonishing how lifelike the images are, is it not?"

Cecily felt like screaming. Why was Miss Braithwaite speaking and not Papa, who was surely the one who ought to be having a conversation with Rosalind? Rosalind said, "I have brought with me a portrait I made of Cecily recently…as a gift for the whole family but most of all for you, Cecily."

She reached into her bag and took out something about the same size as a book, but flat. "It's Cecily posing as Miranda, from *The Tempest*."

Papa took the proffered image and Cecily went to stand beside him to have a look.

"Oh!" she said, lost for words. Was this really her? Could it be? Cecily had seen some other photographs that Rosalind had taken of her, and had grown more used to seeing her own image magically transported to a piece of stiff paper. But this portrait was beautiful. She looked quite unlike herself in some ways and very like in others. She was staring towards the edge of the frame. Her hair seemed to be streaming out behind her, because of the skilful way Rosalind had arranged it on the cloak. In the background, the painting of rocks and seashore looked wonderfully lifelike, and Cecily was amazed by the emotions that the expression on her face conveyed: she was sad and full of longing, and looking towards the horizon as though she expected something astonishing to be there, in the distance, almost out of reach. "Thank you!" she added, rather inadequately, and Rosalind smiled at her.

"You are very welcome," she said.

"It's a remarkable portrait, Miss Templeton," said Papa. "I am very grateful and it will have pride of place in the parlour, I promise you. I am more than ever convinced that Cecily's idea of a family portrait as a gift for my sister is a good one."

He placed the photograph on the mantelpiece and Miss Braithwaite made some indistinct noises meant to convey approval. Sam, bored after too many minutes of grown-ups talking, had started to kick the carpet with the toes of his shoes. Cecily said, "May I take Sam to the nursery?"

"An excellent suggestion," Papa replied, and Miss Braithwaite turned to Rosalind and added, "Cecily is so good with her little brother. She's a great help to her father."

Rosalind said, "Sam, dear, I will come up and see your nursery when I've finished talking to your papa. Agreed?"

Sam nodded, then ran to Rosalind and flung his arms around her and kissed her on the cheek.

"Why, Samuel!" Miss Braithwaite said. "I'm sure Miss Templeton doesn't wish to be mauled in that fashion."

Sam said, "What's mauling? I'm kissing Miss Templeton because she's so pretty!"

Laughter followed the children out of the room. "Clever Sam!" Cecily hugged her brother. She felt certain that Miss Braithwaite would not have been pleased by Sam's behaviour. She'd visited their house on many occasions and her brother had shown not the slightest interest in kissing her. Cecily didn't think Sam had ever exchanged more than a couple of words with Miss Braithwaite.

"Will Rosalind come and see us?" Sam wanted to know.

"She said she would, so she will," Cecily answered, but part of her worried that she might forget, or else be held fast in the drawing room by Miss Braithwaite. She could not stop thinking of the picture of herself as Miranda. This image pleased her better than any other she had seen, and Rosalind must have liked it too, to choose it for a gift. It occurred to her that perhaps Rosalind had chosen the picture because Miranda, like

Cecily, was motherless. Maybe that was why it was such a successful portrait: because she herself had felt at ease pretending to be that particular heroine.

CHAPTER NINE

Rosalind and the Doll's House

"And this," said Rosalind, "must be the dining room. How lovely!"

She'd sat down on the carpet to look more carefully at the doll's house, without giving any thought to what might become of her dress. Cecily knew that Rosalind was careless of her clothes, as her blouses were frequently marked with paint, or a streak of colour from one of her props. Once, when Cecily had stared at a pale streak of chalk on the sleeve of one of her garments, Rosalind had smiled and said: "It'll come out in the wash, Cecily…it's of no consequence at all." She'd added, "I never care how I look, only how what I'm looking at looks. That's a great many 'looks' in one sentence, is it not?" and then they'd laughed together.

"This is," she told the children, "a very fine house indeed. Did you say your papa had made it?"

Cecily nodded. "I helped him, too," she said. "I stuck the wallpaper on in most of the rooms. Papa brushed the back of the paper with paste, and I held the pieces against the walls."

"The clothes are so well-made! Who made those?"

"My Aunt Lizzie…the one we're making the portrait for. She's very clever with her needle."

Sam held out the toy soldier he was clutching to Cecily. "Can General Bones come and sleep in the doll's house?" he said.

"He can go in the guest room," said Cecily. "Put him there."

While Sam was settling his general into the empty bed in the guest room, Rosalind said, "If you'd like them, I've some scraps left of a lovely new wallpaper …my bedroom was redecorated last year. It's a pattern from Mr. William Morris's factory called *Willow*…"

"New paper?" Cecily was taken aback. She'd never imagined that anything in the doll's house would change, but it *was* true that the paper was a little shabby and coming away from the corners in some rooms. How wonderful if her doll's house could share the same paper as Rosalind's bedroom! She said, "Thank you! I'd love that."

Rosalind wanted to know the names of each and every one of the da Pontes. After Cecily had recited them, she added, "My parents went to Venice on their honeymoon, and the da Pontes were a real family they met there."

Rosalind nodded. "I don't think you ever grow out of doll's houses, do you? I love them, and this one is particularly fine. I had one myself, but it's in the attic now. Such a pity. Perhaps I'll take you up there one day…" She moved Mama da Ponte from her place at the head of the tiny table to an armchair in the drawing room and took Paolo and Maggie into the nursery where she laid them in their beds.

Sam was growing impatient. "Have you finished looking at the doll's house? I want to go in the garden now."

"Oh, Sam, why the garden? There's nothing for Rosalind to see there," Cecily said. How tiresome little brothers could be! Just as she and Rosalind were beginning to talk about personal matters. She felt that within a few minutes, the subject of her dead mama might have come up and she could have poured out her heart to such a sympathetic listener! Now here was Sam, distracting Rosalind. Perhaps she'd say she had no desire to see anything outdoors?

Cecily stifled a sigh, but before she could say anything more, Rosalind had taken Sam's hand and jumped up, smoothing down her skirts.

"Delightful! Cecily, there's no need for you to come if you'd rather stay here or go back to the drawing room. Sam will show me everything, I'm sure, and we'll be back very soon."

"Very well." Cecily knew that she oughtn't to feel jealous of her brother, but she did. Why, she asked herself as they left the nursery, doesn't Rosalind ask me to go as well? Is she tired of my company? Does she like Sam better than she likes me? She kneeled down beside the doll's house and moved Papa da Ponte out of the kitchen – who had placed him there? – and put him to sit next to his wife. Most of the time, when she played with the dolls, she was soothed by them and they made her feel more cheerful, so why could she not concentrate on their lives now? It was, she knew, because she wanted to be down in the garden with Sam and Rosalind and hadn't had the grace to say so when she had the chance.

I can go there now, she thought, and ran to the window. Looking out, she could see most of the lawn.

Sam and Rosalind were under the walnut tree… Sam won't tell Rosalind about Aunt Lizzie and how she'd grown it from a nut, Cecily thought. She made her way quickly downstairs and out of the back door. The sun was shining now, and Cecily put her hand up to shade her eyes from the brightness.

"Sam! Are you climbing? You know you're not allowed to, when Papa isn't there to watch you."

"I am! I can!" Sam cried. Rosalind was looking up at him. He'd clambered on to the lowest branch and had put out a hand to reach for another, slightly higher one. He stretched out, standing on the tips of his toes. He can't do it, Cecily thought, staring at him. If he puts a foot out and tries to get up there, he'll fall. She felt herself turning cold all over. Should she shout at him not to move? Go and stand under the tree? Move to help him? Perhaps if she climbed up too, she could persuade him to come down with her… All this went through her mind in seconds and before she could decide what was best, Sam fell from the tree.

"Oh, oh Sam, dear!" Cecily shouted and began to run to where her brother was lying, very still…too still…on the ground. Before she could reach him, Rosalind was there, cradling the little boy's head in her lap and smoothing his brow.

"Sam?" she said. "Sam, open your eyes, dearest! Come now, where are you hurt?"

"I haven't hurt myself," Sam said and sat up. "My foot's a bit sore, but I'm not a baby." Cecily was so relieved to hear him speaking, and in a voice that sounded quite normal, that she burst into tears. "Cecily's the baby!" Sam said triumphantly.

"She most certainly is not! She was worried about you," Rosalind said. "And so was I. There's nothing broken, I hope?" She began to run her hands over Sam's arms and legs, to check that they were indeed unhurt.

"Papa will be so angry!" Cecily said. "You know you're not allowed to climb the tree when Papa is absent. You know that very well."

"You won't do it again, will you, Sam?" Rosalind leaned down to hear Sam's reply. He was now standing up, looking a little shaken. "I think we ought to go inside, don't you?"

Nanny Mildred appeared at the garden door just then, and bustled as quickly as she could to where Rosalind and Sam were standing. "Have you been up that tree again, young man?" she said, frowning. "You are naughty, indeed you are! What have I told you about climbing up there? Come along now…come with me to the nursery this minute."

She took Sam's hand and almost dragged him away. He looked back at Rosalind as he went, and waved happily at her.

"Poor Sam!" Rosalind said. "But this walnut tree is so beautiful. Maybe we could pose the family here for your portrait, if the day is fine?"

"Oh, that would be wonderful! I should have thought of that myself. My Aunt Lizzie planted the tree when she was a girl. The year my father was born…"

"How very appropriate! I will consult with your father of course. I think he's expecting an indoor photograph, and we discussed the possibility of his study, but this will be much more…interesting. The light outside…" She examined the tree with renewed interest.

"Sam really likes you, you know," Cecily said. "Look, he's waving to us from the nursery window."

"I'm very pleased he does," Rosalind said, waving back. "He's a lovely child." Cecily said nothing and Rosalind, noticing her silence, put an arm around her shoulders and squeezed her close. "And you, Cecily, are lovely too…you know I think that, do you not?"

Cecily nodded, feeling happiness spread through her as though it were a growing plant. If only Rosalind could stay here for ever, she thought. If only we had a mother like her, Sam and I. She thought this, and as she did, an idea came into her mind.

CHAPTER TEN

The Bright Family Photograph

"…and it isn't just me, Amy. Sam thinks almost the same thing, even though I've not spoken to him about it. I know he'd love Rosalind to be our mother."

Cecily and Amy were sitting under the walnut tree in the garden of Number Six, Chelsea Walk. Nanny Mildred had forbidden all climbing among its branches, but as the girls were busily occupied making a daisy chain, and talking about Cecily's latest idea, this was no hardship. Amy said, "But Cecily, it's a ridiculous daydream. Why on earth should Rosalind want to be your mother?"

Cecily decided to ignore the rudeness of her friend's remark, which meant, as far as she could see, that Amy considered being a mother in the Bright household a less than pleasant task. "Why," she said, "anyone would think Sam and I are horrid children. You don't think so, do you, Amy?"

"No, of course I don't, but I'm your friend. Someone who isn't accustomed to you both might have a different opinion. You want your papa to fall in love with Rosalind, don't you? And she with him."

"Yes," Cecily admitted. She imagined her papa and Rosalind, sitting in armchairs beside the fire in the drawing room, with herself and Sam at their feet, and chided herself for her daydream. But Amy's remarks were often double-edged. Cecily didn't know whether to feel relieved that Amy had said she was her friend, or offended because she'd managed to imply that she'd had to grow "accustomed" to Cecily before she became one. She'd also made it sound as though Papa and Rosalind falling in love was so unlikely as to be all but impossible.

Amy continued, "You said Miss Braithwaite was there when Rosalind came to your house?"

Cecily nodded, miserably. "She behaved as if she was the mistress of the house. She poured the tea. She stood at the door to say goodbye to Rosalind when the time came for her to go home. She and Papa stood arm in arm."

"Then all is lost," said Amy, using her fingernails to nip a daisy through its fat stalk. "Rosalind probably thinks Miss Braithwaite is your father's fiancée."

"Then I shall tell her the truth. That Papa and Miss Braithwaite are friends and no more."

"Are you quite sure that they aren't more than friends?"

This made Cecily pause in alarm. "I don't think they are. Papa does not act as though he loves her. Not at all. I am sure I would see something in his manner. Don't people behave…well, not as they usually do… when they're in love? And besides, you were the one who said Miss Braithwaite was too plain for someone to fall in love with."

"I did say that, it's true, but I think I might have been wrong. If you look about you at married people, they are often far from beautiful, aren't they? It's possible," Amy suggested, putting the daisy chain over her head so that it hung down almost to her waist, "that they want to hide their devotion from you. They might wish to keep it a secret."

"My papa would never keep a secret from me," Cecily said firmly and Amy smiled.

"You think he wouldn't," she said, "but he would. All grown-ups keep secrets from us. They don't even think of it as keeping secrets. They just say: *we mustn't tell the children* and think they're doing it for our good."

"Stop! You're making me feel gloomy!" Cecily said. "I'm going to try and bring my papa and Rosalind together as much as I can. She's so pretty that he's bound to fall in love with her, don't you think? If he sees her often, he'll get used to her and think of her as a friend."

"I thought you said he was rather cold when he spoke to her."

"He was at first," Cecily said, "but now that she's visited the house, he'll be more cordial, I'm sure."

"But," said Amy, "what will happen if he starts to like *her* better but she will have none of *him*? Perhaps your papa isn't to her taste. Are you certain she hasn't a beau we know nothing about?"

Cecily fell back on to the grass, not caring that there would probably be green marks all over her white blouse and Nanny would scold her and Florrie would make tutting noises as she took it downstairs with the laundry. There were little scraps of blue sky visible through the leaves of the walnut tree and Cecily blinked hard to stop herself from crying. What Amy said must be true. Why had she not realized it herself?

Of course someone as lovely as Rosalind must have any number of young men in pursuit of her…oh, it was so dreadfully disappointing! Rosalind would never become a mother to her and Sam and that was that.

Amy left the garden a little while later and it was only after she'd gone home that something else occurred to Cecily: how did her friend dare to suggest that Papa wouldn't be to Rosalind's taste? Anyone could see that he was handsome and kind and ever so much younger than portly Mr. Chistlehurst, who looked just like Humpty Dumpty, with his bald head and round stomach. So there, Cecily said to herself, knowing that she'd never have spoken out loud if her friend had been there to hear. Amy was probably jealous because Cecily had a father who was far superior in every possible way.

"A little to the left, Cecily, if you please…"

Cecily moved nearer to her father. Rosalind was arranging her and Papa and Sam before taking the family photograph. She had visited the house twice more, since the Sunday when Sam had fallen out of the walnut tree. Rosalind and Papa had talked most pleasantly on each occasion, and Ellen Braithwaite had been absent, which made Cecily feel that perhaps there might be hope for her impossible dream.

They were out in the garden, and fortunately the day was sunny, with high, white clouds drifting across the sky. Rosalind had set up her tripod on the lawn and Cecily noticed that she'd brought her smaller camera with her. A white wrought-iron chair and table had been moved from their usual place beside the trellis to a shady spot under the walnut tree and Papa had been directed to sit down and look as though he were about to drink a pleasant cup of tea in the open air.

"Not," Rosalind told him, "as though you were about to be sentenced by a particularly harsh judge to a very long jail sentence." That had made Papa smile, which was, Cecily knew, exactly what Rosalind had intended. Cecily was behind him, leaning over his right shoulder and Sam was on Papa's left, with Papa's arm around him, which would look delightful and had the added advantage of keeping her young brother in position while the photograph was being taken. Mossy had wandered over to the table to see what was happening, and Cecily wondered whether perhaps composing the photograph might take so long that she'd feel like jumping on the table and would maybe even fall asleep there, but her hopes were in vain. The silly cat, quite unaware of the importance of this picture, decided that more amusement was to be had chasing a stray leaf that was whirling about in the breeze, and off she went in pursuit of it. Well, thought Cecily, she won't be in the family portrait but that can't be helped.

"Now, Sam, stand very still, please," Rosalind said, her voice muffled from her position under the black cloth, and Papa added, "I fear you're asking the impossible, Miss Templeton."

"Please call me *Rosalind*. Miss Templeton sounds like someone's rather strict teacher."

"I feel that would be a little... We hardly know one another."

"On the contrary, I know you very well, Mr. Bright. I always learn a great deal about someone I'm photographing."

Papa was blushing! Cecily could scarcely believe it. Oh, I wish I could tell Amy! she thought. Surely blushing means *something*? It might only have been embarrassment, but there was hope it might be something else, Cecily felt sure.

"That's perfect, Cecily. Now try to look into the camera as though something you like a great deal is there, in the lens... That's right, Sam...some wonderful thing...another cat...a dog...a train."

"Yes, a train!" said Sam and he was on the point of setting out across the lawn making steam-engine noises when Papa, gripping him even more tightly round the shoulders, said, "Do not move, Sam!

Rosalind has said you must be still and we are at her mercy."

"Thank you, Mr. Bright. I'm grateful for your help. Ready?" She emerged from under the black cloth, and slid the film into the camera. "Do not move for a moment," she said and squeezed the bulb to take the photograph.

Cecily became a statue. She gazed into the round darkness of the lens. She tried to imagine what Rosalind was seeing. I wish I could look through the lens and take a picture myself. How strange I must look, upside down! She thought about the occasion, a few days ago when she'd been allowed into the darkroom for the first time. What a magical and mysterious thing it was, to see the picture emerge gradually when the plate was dipped and soaked in the strange-smelling chemicals! Developers, emulsion, fixers… Cecily hadn't been allowed to touch anything, but she looked and looked and tried to keep everything in her mind to think about when she was alone.

Soon, there was a small click and it was all over. Rosalind smiled. "That was lovely. I'm grateful, Mr. Bright, for your cooperation. I will try to make a delightful present for your sister and I will call on you soon to show you the finished portrait."

"John, I think," Papa said, taking Rosalind's hand. "If you are not to be Miss Templeton, then I can't be Mr. Bright."

Cecily concentrated on watching her father to see how he appeared and it seemed to her that he was speaking in much warmer tones than he had before. He smiled as he looked at Rosalind. Was he just happy, pleased that the sitting had gone well? Or was his affection growing?

"Very well," said Rosalind. "John it will be."

At that moment, the garden door opened and Miss Braithwaite came across the lawn almost at a run, looking much more animated than she normally did. She started speaking even as she approached the spot where Papa and Rosalind were standing.

"Oh, dear Miss Templeton, how sorry I am that I've missed the sitting! I did so want to be in attendance! I'm mortified that I wasn't here to greet you."

Rosalind murmured an answer, which Cecily didn't hear because she was looking at her father. He had stepped away from Rosalind, as though he was a little ashamed of being caught standing so close to her. Miss Braithwaite was now whispering in Rosalind's ear. Rosalind was frowning. She said, "I'm so sorry... I would need to arrange a special sitting, Miss Braithwaite, for that."

"For what, my dear?" Papa asked.

"Why, John, I have asked whether Miss Templeton might take a photograph of the two of us!"

Cecily felt as though she might faint. Oh, please, she thought. Not that. Anything but that... How could Miss Braithwaite suggest such a thing? What will Papa say? If he says he'd like that, Rosalind will definitely think they have an understanding.

Then Papa said, "We have kept Miss Rosalind for far

too long this afternoon. She must be anxious to return to her own house…perhaps another day."

Thank goodness, Cecily thought, closing her eyes in relief. Thank goodness for that. Next time I see Rosalind alone, I'll tell her that Miss Braithwaite is simply a good friend of the family. And I'll try to find out whether there are any young men calling on Rosalind. She was still wondering whether she could ask her such a thing directly, when Papa and Rosalind and Miss Braithwaite went back into the house together.

CHAPTER ELEVEN

Cecily is Puzzled

Cecily was so excited that she could hardly hold her pen steady and she had already made several blots of ink on the paper. Never mind…

…*You will soon be with us, dear Aunt Lizzie!* she wrote. *Sam and I are so excited we can hardly bear to wait another two weeks. I have very little to write about because everything I want to tell you is VERY SECRET and cannot be revealed…*

Cecily paused, put her pen aside and gazed out of the window. She was looking forward to Aunt Lizzie's visit, but what was the point of writing to her when there was so little she could tell? Several days had gone by since Rosalind took their picture and although Papa had given permission for Cecily to visit the Templetons on two occasions, there had been no opportunity to find out more about whether or not Rosalind had a beau, nor discover what her opinion of Papa was. Cecily had mentioned that Miss Braithwaite was just a friend of the family, but Rosalind seemed eager to change the subject. Meanwhile, Miss Braithwaite visited almost every day, and once or twice she told them when she arrived that she had "passed that nice Mr. Templeton and exchanged a few words with him".

This made Cecily very gloomy. She was quite sure that Mr. Templeton would tell his daughter of these encounters and she would think that Miss Braithwaite was constantly visiting Number Six, Chelsea Walk, which was quite true. Cecily wished she could speak to Rosalind about it all, but was not sure what else she could say.

"Cecily, dear," said Nanny Mildred, sounding rather flustered as she came into the nursery. "You must come downstairs at once. Miss Templeton is here with the photograph. Please go and find Sam. He's in the garden I believe."

Cecily flew to the open window and saw Sam lying on the grass, trying to tempt Mossy into chasing a stick, when she was intent on hunting butterflies.

"Sam!" she called. "Rosalind's come to show us the photograph. Come inside and see."

He jumped up at once and Cecily turned to leave the nursery. Nanny Mildred shook her head. "Well, really, how common! Calling out of the window like that! If I'd wanted someone to call out of the window, I might have done so myself. You should know better, Cecily. Such behaviour is far from ladylike."

"Never mind, Nanny dear!" said Cecily, smiling happily. "I was excited, that's all. Will you come down and look at the photograph?"

"I daresay," said Nanny Mildred, allowing herself to be wheedled into a better temper. "It's a fine thing, this photography. My niece has had a portrait done to mark her engagement… She is going to send me a copy."

"You must show me, Nanny! I would love to see it when it comes."

Papa was sitting at his desk when Cecily went into the study. Sam was holding Rosalind's hand. Rosalind was standing beside Papa and pointing at the photograph.

"Ah, Cecily, come and have a look," said Papa. "It's most astonishing…most unsettling too, to see oneself portrayed like this…fixed on paper for ever. And you children too. Come and see. Miss Rosalind has worked wonders with her enchanted box."

Papa had asked for the photograph to be framed. This made the picture look like one of Mr. Templeton's and much grander than many of the photographs Cecily had seen, which were simply mounted on dark grey cardboard. She stared down at the three of them: herself, Papa and Sam. I know Papa and Sam better than anyone, she thought, and myself too, but we look…she couldn't decide how to describe the way they appeared in the image on the desk.

I'm quite pretty, Cecily thought, and she immediately blushed at her own vanity. She had seen herself as Cinderella, as Miranda, as Cecily from Mr. Wilde's play but never before had she looked at a photograph of herself as who she truly was. Her dress seemed to glow with the sunlight that fell on it through the leaves of the walnut tree, and the folds of her skirt were so clear that you felt you could reach in and touch the fabric. Sam was smiling. How happy he looked! His hair fell on to his brow and his eyes were shining. Papa…well, Papa looked very handsome. His hand, resting on the table in front of him, was so lifelike that you felt it had just stopped moving. Rosalind had composed the photograph so that the three of them were framed in an arch of branches and she'd made sure that the shadows made by the sun shining through the leaves fell in such a way as not to spoil the image. That's the most important part, Cecily thought. Finding the right picture to begin with: the exact right way to remember everything.

"It's lovely!" she said. "Aunt Lizzie will love it."

Papa stood up and said, "Rosalind, I cannot thank you enough. When Cecily came to me with this idea, I was doubtful, I confess. But you have made us all look…well…" He glanced down at his feet and he was, Cecily was glad to see, blushing again. She knew her father was not good at being fulsome, but he was clearly very pleased. He went on, "You've made us look very fine, and the tree looks magnificent, which I know will please my sister greatly. I would be delighted…more than delighted…if you would join us for the party on Lizzie's birthday. You and your father too, of course. May 18th is the day. We will be outdoors, if the weather permits, and I shall present her with this gift. Perhaps, if you wouldn't mind bringing your camera with you, you might photograph my sister, too… Would that spoil the day for you? I don't want you to feel you are working when everyone else is celebrating."

"I never feel that taking photographs is work," Rosalind said, smiling at Papa. "And I like bringing my camera outdoors more than anything. I'm interested in light, you see. I enjoy seeing whether the camera can match the paintbrush when it comes to giving an impression of a scene. I admire the Impressionists very much, as you know, but I think my little wooden box does very well. So thank you…that would be delightful. I must go home now," Rosalind said.

"Then please allow me to accompany you," Papa said.

Cecily could hardly believe her ears. Rosalind had said: "as you know". This meant that she'd spoken to Papa already about her tastes in art. When had they spoken? Cecily had heard no such conversation. Was it possible that Rosalind and Papa had had a private talk Cecily knew nothing about? When? How? And now her father was offering to take Rosalind home. Did this mean…could it mean…that they were better friends than Cecily knew? Might they become *even* better friends? Might they… Before she could finish the thought, Sam spoke up, "I want to come too! I want to go with Rosalind and Papa."

"Of course you may come, dear," Rosalind said. "And Cecily too, if you'd like to, though of course I need no such accompaniment. It is only a short distance to my house, after all."

"Nevertheless, you will have a Bright family escort," said Papa and Cecily realized that he was trying to be light-hearted. She looked to see whether he was hiding his disappointment, but he seemed to be quite cheerful.

Florrie had just closed the door behind them, and they were going down the front steps to the street, when Miss Braithwaite suddenly appeared at the gate.

"How do you all do!" she shrilled. "I am a little late,

it seems, for you seem to be on your way somewhere."

"We're taking Rosalind home to her house!" Sam cried and Miss Braithwaite said, "How charming! I trust I can join the procession!"

She took Papa's arm and everyone set out towards the Templetons'. Cecily was so angry that she could feel her teeth grinding together. How could Papa and Rosalind ever grow more familiar with one another if Miss Braithwaite made such a show of being his special friend? And how did it happen that she always appeared at exactly the wrong moment? It was enough to make a person weep with frustration. I shall have to talk to Amy about it, she decided.

The next day or two passed very slowly. Amy was in bed with a heavy cold and sore throat and Mrs. Chistlehurst had forbidden all visitors. Cecily didn't mind at first, even though it meant she could not talk about what Rosalind had said (*I love the Impressionists, as you know…*) and what it might mean. How did Papa know such a thing? Cecily didn't wish to catch any germs, so she was waiting for Amy to feel well enough for a visit. She spent her time meanwhile drawing at the nursery table and playing with the da Pontes and when the weather was fine, sitting on a cushion under the walnut tree with Mr. Lewis Carroll's book, *Alice's Adventures in Wonderland*.

Now she was standing at the drawing-room window, waiting for Papa to come home. He was rather late, as he had been yesterday and the day before that, and Cecily supposed that there must be a great deal of work to do at his office. She gazed out into the road, not really looking for him, but wondering if she might see his approach. She noticed two figures in the distance: a man and a woman, walking together. I wish that Papa and Rosalind might walk home like that, she thought, but it seems as if they never will. She hadn't visited the Templetons' house since the photograph had been delivered and she decided that this very evening she would ask Papa for permission.

The couple was coming closer now and she could make out…could it be? Cecily brought her face so close to the window that her breath misted the glass. It was! It was Papa and Rosalind was at his side. He was standing close to her, and now he was taking her hand… and she was saying something to him. Now he'd turned to walk home, and she began to walk in the opposite direction, going towards her house. Where had they come from? Could they have met somewhere and walked to Chelsea together? Had they met by accident? Should she ask Papa when he came in? Or Rosalind? She wished more than anything that Amy was there to talk to. Papa and Rosalind alone together… However the meeting came about, surely it meant *something*?

"I am quite sure," said Cecily. She and Amy were in the Chistlehursts' morning room. Amy had been allowed a visitor at last, but Mrs. Chistlehurst insisted that she stay indoors, even though the weather was fine. "I know what I saw. He was bending over her hand. I never saw him do that to Miss Braithwaite. And he invited her to Aunt Lizzie's party. And he knew she liked the Impressionists. How did he find that out, if he has never been alone with her? She hasn't spoken about such things when I've been with them."

"He's been calling on her and not telling you," Amy said. "They've probably met at an art gallery and looked at paintings together."

"Then that means he likes her, doesn't it?"

"I think it's most romantic… Perhaps they will elope."

"That's stupid. Why would they need to elope? No one is stopping them from seeing one another."

"There's Miss Braithwaite, though. Don't forget her."

Cecily buried her face in her hands. "I like forgetting about her, Amy. But why should she make any difference to what Papa does?"

Amy considered. After a while she delivered her verdict. "Perhaps your papa *does* have an understanding with Miss Braithwaite. Indeed, perhaps he's asked her to marry him. Have you thought of that?"

"Oh, no…he'd never…surely he wouldn't? She's so dull. He couldn't. Could he?"

"Yes, he could. And the reason he's not spoken about it to you is because he knows what you think of her…and he's plucking up his courage."

"But what about Rosalind?"

"Rosalind," said Amy triumphantly, "truly *is* just a friend, but your papa is keeping their friendship secret out of consideration for his betrothed, who'd be most put out if she found out that he was going to art galleries with another lady. I'm sure I must be right."

What could Cecily say to contradict Amy's version of what was happening? It all seemed to fit the case perfectly, and she wondered what, if anything, she could do to stop her father making such a mistake. Perhaps she might ask Aunt Lizzie. She was always very sensible, but would she want to be plunged into the depths of this problem right in the midst of her birthday visit?

CHAPTER TWELVE

The Birthday Party

"I see that my birthday weather is going to be perfect," said Aunt Lizzie. She was in the nursery with Cecily and Sam, having been banished from the kitchen by Cook, and asked to stay out of the drawing room while Florrie arranged the flowers which had been delivered very early that morning.

Aunt Lizzie was already dressed for the party. Cecily looked at her as she stood next to Sam by the window and thought that although no one could call her a beauty, and although she was celebrating her fiftieth birthday, she was very handsome: tall and slim and always with a smile on her face. Others (like Amy) might think her complexion had seen too much of the sun, from her work outdoors, but Cecily thought she looked splendid in a periwinkle-blue dress, which had been bought for this day.

The sandwiches, some filled with sliced cucumber and some with poached fresh salmon and all looking dainty with their crusts cut off, were ready in the larder. The cakes had been baked and were ready on the cake stands, and neighbours had lent the Brights their garden chairs to accommodate the guests. Florrie had enlisted the help of some of the staff from other houses in Chelsea Walk to assist with handing round the food and drink. Twenty visitors were expected and would be arriving very soon. They would take tea and cordial and other refreshments from a long table that had been set out at the bottom of the garden.

Papa and Aunt Lizzie and the children had eaten luncheon at the morning-room table ("Not a proper luncheon, but just a stopgap till this afternoon," said Cook) so as not to get in the way. Mossy, who had decided that she did not approve of so much disturbance, disappeared early in the morning and Sam, after a long search, found her in the Mouse Hole Room as he called it: the room where they'd found the antique card hidden behind the panelling. She was curled up on one of the beds, almost invisible in the folds of the dust sheet.

"Lizzie?" Papa came into the nursery. "Are you ready to come down to the drawing room? We have a gift for you, and I should like to give it to you before our guests arrive."

"Certainly," said Aunt Lizzie and Cecily took her hand and pulled her to the door.

"At last!" she said. "Come on, Aunt Lizzie. We've been so longing to show you…"

"I'm not allowed to say yet, am I, Cecily?" That was

Sam and Cecily whirled round immediately and put her hand over her brother's mouth.

"No…oh, no, Sam. Don't utter a squeak."

This made Sam laugh and he started squeaking at once. Cecily wished she'd said something else. She'd spent the last few days impressing on her brother the importance of complete secrecy and silence, but since Aunt Lizzie's arrival last night, she'd made it her business not to leave Sam alone with her even for one moment. He'd been very good so far, but she was determined not to take her eyes off him until the photograph was safely in Aunt Lizzie's hand.

In the drawing room, Papa handed the parcel to Aunt Lizzie. She looked at it and turned it over once or twice.

"Not a book, I think. And not any kind of plant, I'm quite sure. Perhaps…could it be…?"

"Open it, Aunt Lizzie!" Sam cried. "Open it now."

"Very well." Aunt Lizzie sat down in an armchair and began to unwrap the package. When the photograph was revealed, she gasped and turned bright red and Cecily saw that there were tears standing in her eyes.

"How beautiful! All my loved ones! And under the walnut tree. Oh, it's so wonderful! How…when…you must have…"

Now that the secret was revealed, Sam flung himself at Aunt Lizzie and said, "Rosalind took our photograph. We had to stand so still. And Mossy didn't want to, so she's not in the picture. This is me, can you see? Does it look like me?"

"It looks just like you, dear boy! And like Cecily and you, too, John. I am overwhelmed. Truly. I never expected such a fine gift. I will treasure it for ever. And who is Rosalind?"

"She's the photographer who took the picture. Rosalind Templeton. Her father is the well-known painter, Roderick Templeton. She has a very good eye, I think," said Papa. "You will meet both her and her father this afternoon. She wishes to take some photographs of you most particularly, Lizzie."

"Oh, no, I could never…I'm not…"

"Nonsense, Lizzie. I won't hear a word of objection. Have you thought how much we would like an image of you to remind us of what you look like when you're down in Sussex?"

Aunt Lizzie hugged the framed photograph to her bosom. "If you put it like that, I suppose you are right. The day will come when everyone will have photographs at hand of everything they wish to see… It's like magic, is it not? Thank you, all of you. More than I can say."

The afternoon sunshine lay in golden stripes across the lawn. The guests had marvelled at the photographic equipment, eaten the food provided, and talked and laughed. Cecily was quite surprised to be approached by Mr. Templeton, who seemed to be waving his sandwich aloft, as though it were a flag.

"Cecily my dear," he said. "D'you remember how

I met you shortly after attending the first night of Mr. Wilde's play, *The Importance of Being Earnest*? I believe I told you then that one of the heroines was a Cecily, did I not?"

"You did, sir," said Cecily, still puzzled.

"Cucumber sandwiches figure in the play as well… They are quite a feature in their own way, in the very first scene! How remarkable!"

He ambled off across the grass, lost in thought and now eating the sandwich instead of flourishing it above his head. Rosalind was sitting down quite near the house with her camera at her side and Cecily went over to stand next to her.

"I think," Rosalind said, "that you should be the one to take the photograph of your Aunt Lizzie."

"Really? You'd let me do that? Oh, how lovely… I would love to! But is there enough light? It's getting quite late."

"No, the light will do very well. I've seen how interested you are in the process, and you've seen how I work... I can help you. You'd enjoy taking this photograph, wouldn't you?"

Cecily was speechless and could only nod her head. Rosalind went off to fetch Aunt Lizzie. How wonderfully everything was turning out! Rosalind understood Cecily's longing to be the person behind the camera, the one who saw the image upside down and covered her head to compose the picture and make sure the focus was true and clear. The one who decided which single moment, from all the possible moments at this point in someone's life, should be the one that lasted for ever.

"What's this, Cecily?" Aunt Lizzie came over quickly with Rosalind following behind her. "This is the time for that photograph of me that you mentioned? I'm very excited at the prospect...and honoured...and *you're* going to take it, I believe. Such a treat!"

"Will you please stand there, Aunt Lizzie? Next to that branch that slants down a little...that's right. You have to be very still."

Cecily let Rosalind cover her head with the cloth.

"When you look through the lens and see something that you think would make a good picture, Cecily, come out and then slide the film in and just squeeze this bulb…so." She put the bulb into Cecily's hand where it felt rubbery and smooth. She did what Rosalind had told her to and peered into the lens and there was Aunt Lizzie, upside down but still recognizable. It was strange, but somehow Cecily could tell how the image would appear when it was the right way up… Aunt Lizzie was smiling. Her face was in shadow, and there were sprinklings of sunshine on her skirt. Were they too bright? Would they spoil the picture? No, that would do very well. She emerged from beneath the cloth and took a deep breath. She slid the film in carefully and squeezed the bulb. There was general applause, and Aunt Lizzie smiled.

"Thank you," she said. "I'll look forward to seeing this picture…very much."

She bent nearer to Cecily and whispered in her ear.

"You look so happy, dearest child."

"I am, I really am, Aunt Lizzie. More than anything, I wish I could be a photographer when I grow up."

"Then I'm sure you will be. I've always believed that if you want something enough, you should try your hardest to achieve it. And those who try hard very often succeed."

Amy ran over to Cecily and asked her how she'd felt, looking at the world from under a stifling black cloth. *How can I possibly explain how exciting it was?* Cecily asked herself. She didn't have the words to express what she felt, so said only, "It was strange but I liked it." She wondered how soon it would be before she looked through the camera lens again.

Most of the guests had gone, but a few were still left, sitting on chairs in the shade of the house, chatting to Aunt Lizzie. All the friends she'd known when she lived in Number Six, Chelsea Walk had come and they'd brought every kind of gift, but not one of them (so Aunt Lizzie told Sam, and Cecily had overheard them) was as delightful as the photograph of the Bright family.

Amy and all the Chistlehursts had gone home. So had Mr. Templeton because he was expected at an evening gathering in Mayfair. Miss Braithwaite was hovering near Papa, and Cecily stopped feeling relieved that she'd spent the afternoon speaking to other guests for the most part. Cecily and Sam were now sitting under the walnut tree and Mossy had been tempted out by the smell of the salmon in the sandwiches. She'd found a few morsels on the grass and eaten them, and was now fast asleep on Cecily's lap.

"Try very hard not to move, Cecily and Sam." Rosalind was there, a little to their left, and she had moved up on them so quietly that they hadn't noticed. "I'm going to take a picture of you both as you are now…such lovely patterns of light and shade on your dress, Cecily. This image will be dappled all over with light…just like an Impressionist painting…"

Cecily sat as still as she could. While she was not moving, she noticed that Miss Braithwaite had now attached herself to Papa and was clinging to his arm and leaning against him in a very familiar way. As soon as I can move, Cecily thought, as soon as the photograph is taken, I will go over to them and they will have to separate.

"There," said Rosalind. "You may move now, children."

Cecily got to her feet, but Miss Braithwaite was quicker.

"Miss Templeton," she called out to Rosalind. "Please allow me to thank you so much for coming and marking the occasion with your truly wonderful photographs. John, dearest, I've been thinking. Perhaps we may have a picture taken of the three of us, while Miss Templeton is here…you and Lizzie and me. I am, after all, almost a member of the family, am I not?"

Papa looked quite shocked, but said nothing.

Rosalind, Cecily saw, turned very pale. She said, "I would like nothing better, but alas, I have not brought enough supplies… I can only carry a limited amount with me. I'm so sorry. I used my last plate taking the photograph of the children."

"Never mind," said Miss Braithwaite. "There will be another occasion. Perhaps an even happier one than this, I daresay."

She means a wedding, Cecily realized. Does she? Is that what she means? How could that be?

Rosalind said, "I have to go home now. I'm late already. I'll say goodbye to all of you and thank you for a very pleasant afternoon."

She began to pack up her equipment rather hastily. Papa was moving to go with her to the front door, but Miss Braithwaite was there before him.

"I'll show Miss Templeton out, John. You have your other guests to attend to."

"I need no accompaniment, thank you, Miss Braithwaite," said Rosalind. "I will do very well alone."

She was gone so quickly that neither Miss Braithwaite nor Papa could keep up with her. Cecily felt a shadow fall over the whole afternoon.

CHAPTER THIRTEEN

Telling Aunt Lizzie

Aunt Lizzie sat down at the end of Cecily's bed. "I think," she said, "that you should tell me what's wrong. I can see you're not as happy as you were earlier this morning. Has something happened? Did you perhaps have a disagreement with your friend Amy during the party?"

Cecily said, "No, it's not that... It's only..." She didn't know what to say next. Perhaps she ought to keep quiet? But how wonderful it would be to tell someone of her fears and hopes!

"Will you promise not to tell Papa? Promise?"

"I can't promise that, Cecily, but I won't tell him unless I consider it absolutely necessary for him to know. Do you think it will be?"

"No… It's not anything that I couldn't say to him, but…"

"I know. Sometimes it's difficult to talk to those who are closest to you…"

Cecily spoke in a rush because she knew that if she hesitated, she would say nothing at all. "I think Miss Braithwaite wants to be our new mama. I think Papa's going to ask her to marry him and I don't like her and don't want her to live with us. I'd rather have no mother at all, truly. And I hoped that…"

"Yes? What did you hope?"

Could she confess to what she had longed for? Cecily took a deep breath and went on, "I hoped that perhaps Rosalind… Well, she would be a wonderful mother and Sam really likes her and so do I."

"But what about John? Does he like her? Is she more than an acquaintance? He hasn't spoken of her to me."

"I don't know. I saw them standing together in the street, once. Papa has said nothing about her and meanwhile, Miss Braithwaite is constantly here and today…"

Aunt Lizzie stood up. "Go to sleep now, Cecily. I'll speak to John. I shan't say we've had this conversation. And I confess – though now it's your turn to promise not to breathe a word – I've never had a good opinion of Miss Braithwaite. She is pleasant enough but rather tiresome in many ways. Goodnight, Cecily. I shall have to return to Sussex very early in the morning, so I'll say goodbye, too. It's been my best birthday yet. And I look forward to seeing your photograph of me. It will bring back very happy memories." She kissed Cecily on the forehead and said, "Sleep well."

Cecily did not sleep well. She didn't sleep at all for what seemed like a very long time. The grandfather clock on the first-floor landing ticked away the hours and she heard it striking ten o'clock as she lay in her bed, wide awake. She felt warm and pushed back the bedclothes and went to stand at the window. There was a carriage waiting at the gate of Number Six. Someone was speaking in the hall downstairs. Papa was saying goodbye to whoever had ordered the carriage to take them home. Only one person would stay so late…Miss Braithwaite of course. Perhaps, Cecily thought miserably, they've been discussing their wedding plans. If they marry, I will ask to go and live in Sussex with Aunt Lizzie. Would she have me? But what about Sam? I can't leave him, and school and Amy and Papa and everything I know…and I don't want to leave Rosalind.

She crept out onto the landing and went down a few steps so that she had a view of the hall below. Yes, there was Papa and there was Miss Braithwaite, but she was sniffing and holding a handkerchief up to her eyes. Her voice, when she spoke, drifted up to where Cecily was sitting, crouched just below the turn of the stairs and out of sight. I'm eavesdropping, she thought, and felt a little ashamed of herself but not ashamed enough to go back to her room. She listened as hard as she could.

"I was *not* deceiving myself, John," Miss Braithwaite said. "I had every cause for my expectations."

"But I've said nothing." Papa sounded indignant.

"You had no need to say anything. I *knew*. I was such a frequent visitor. We did so much together. You have always been kind and courteous to me. We have so much in common, John. There was no need for you to say the words. I took them for granted."

"Then forgive me, Ellen. You should not have done so. I have never, not once, said I loved you."

"Ah, but can you say you *don't* love me? In all honesty?"

Papa sighed. "I don't love you, Ellen. I'm so sorry…"

"Sorry! I should think so! But sorry doesn't help me. Oh, how will I live? What will I do?"

Miss Braithwaite was wailing now, and wiping away a fresh flood of tears. Cecily tried to feel sorry for her, but she was so happy on her own account that she didn't have any room in her head and heart for kindly feelings towards poor Miss Braithwaite. Papa was consoling her as best he could, while guiding her towards the front door and her carriage.

"We will still be friends," he said to her. "I like you enormously, Ellen, as you must know. I hope you will feel able to visit us sometimes."

"Never!" Miss Braithwaite swept out of the door. "Never again! Farewell for ever, John. I trust you will be happy all alone in this cavernous house." And she was gone and Cecily watched Papa close the door behind her and lean against it, looking exhausted and pale. She crept back to her bedroom and lay in bed, staring at the ceiling. Tomorrow, she thought, I must go and visit Rosalind and tell her Miss Braithwaite is gone. For ever.

Just before she drifted into sleep, she thought: how did Miss Braithwaite dare to call this beautiful house "cavernous"? What a foolish person she is! We shall all be much happier now she's gone.

CHAPTER FOURTEEN

In the Nick of Time

The following morning, Cecily asked permission from Nanny to go and visit the Templetons. She was all ready with stories of how very urgent this visit was, and how she simply had to go, but Nanny was so preoccupied with setting the house in order after the party that she gave her permission at once. Cecily left the house quickly before she could change her mind, and ran to the Templetons' house where she knocked at the door rather more loudly than she'd intended. When Elsie opened it, Cecily asked to speak to Miss Rosalind, urgently.

"Miss Rosalind is packing," said Elsie.

Cecily was silent for a moment. "Why? I mean, please forgive me, but why is she packing?"

"She's going abroad."

"She never told me. She never said anything. Are you quite sure?"

Elsie sighed and stood back from the door. "You'd better come in, Miss Cecily," she said. "You look as though you've lost a sixpence and found a farthing."

"May I see her?"

"I'll ask. You wait here for a moment."

Cecily watched Elsie making her way upstairs and bit her lip to prevent herself from crying. If Rosalind was going abroad so suddenly, there must be a reason. Or maybe she'd been planning the trip for a long time. Cecily pondered this possibility and decided it was impossible. There would have been many opportunities for Rosalind to have said something. Only the other day, she'd been speaking about Venice, and telling Cecily she'd make a good Portia from *The Merchant of Venice*. She would have mentioned it. It looked as though Rosalind was running away, and Cecily wondered whether her flight could have anything to do with Papa. Cecily thought that it must have been the hint about wedding photographs that had upset Rosalind, but surely she couldn't be thinking that Papa was really going to marry Miss Braithwaite? Rosalind must have noticed before how Miss Braithwaite always behaved as though she were already mistress of Number Six, Chelsea Walk, and she knew Miss Braithwaite would be invited to the party, so what must have upset her so much was her belief that Papa was considering an engagement and a wedding. It's lucky that I've come to tell her what Papa said to Miss Braithwaite last night, Cecily thought. I'll let her know that I heard him making it quite clear that he had no intention in the world of ever, ever marrying

Miss Braithwaite and moreover, had never loved her.

"Cecily!" Rosalind came across the hall to her and took both her hands and squeezed them. "Come into the parlour."

Cecily sat in one of the armchairs near the window. Rosalind stood at the mantelpiece. There were violet shadows under her eyes as though she had not slept well. She said, "I'm sorry I said nothing to you yesterday...I was not sure of my plans."

"Did you know you were going abroad?"

"No...no it was something of an impulse. I suddenly felt I wanted to be...well, not here in London, at any rate."

"When will you come back?"

"I don't know. So much depends on...well, never mind."

Cecily had been wondering on her way to the Templeton house how she ought to tell Rosalind about Miss Braithwaite's departure. Should she admit that she had seen Rosalind and Papa together? Should she mention that both she and Sam would be happy to have her as a mother? No, she decided. I'll simply tell her what happened. She said, "Miss Braithwaite won't be visiting us again, I think. She and Papa had a quarrel last night. She told him that she thought he wanted to marry her. She said that she thought he loved her. But he doesn't. He told her so. She was most upset and left in a carriage. She was crying."

Rosalind turned even whiter than she was before, and then her face flushed scarlet. She brought her hand to her mouth and bit her knuckles. She said, "How do you know this? Were you there?"

"I was on the stairs. I couldn't sleep. I went to see who was making such a noise so late at night."

"Did you hear him say that? That he didn't love her?"

"Yes. Yes, I did."

Rosalind sank on to the sofa and tears came to her eyes. "Oh, Cecily...I'm so sorry. I'm behaving like a schoolgirl. I can't help it. I gave up hope yesterday in spite of everything."

"Hope of what?"

"I shouldn't tell you. Your papa said…he said it ought to come from him, but now that you've told me this…"

"I saw you and Papa in the road. Amy said perhaps you'd been to an art gallery together."

"We have met…well, on several occasions since he came to this house when I was photographing you. But there was always Miss Braithwaite in the background."

Cecily's heart began to beat a little faster. "Has… have you and Papa…did you say anything…?"

"No, no, child." Rosalind smiled. "We have discussed many things but not our feelings. He's said nothing that might…well, that might lead me to have any expectations. And then yesterday, with Miss Braithwaite hinting about marriage, I could bear it no longer. I felt I must go…get far away from everything here."

Cecily looked down at her shoes. What did it all mean? Why had Papa not said anything in the least romantic to Rosalind when they'd been together? *I'll* say something, she decided. I'll tell Rosalind. She said, "Sam and I would be so happy if you were our mama. I wish Papa might have fallen in love with you and married you and then we might all have lived together in our house and been happy."

"Oh, Cecily!" Rosalind buried her head in her hands. "I've wished for that too… I fear it will not happen now, for surely a gentleman would have made his feelings known and his intentions clear before now. Even with Miss Braithwaite still on the scene. There were many times when he could have spoken and still he said nothing, though he must have known… Never mind. It's too late now."

"But it's not too late! You don't have to go abroad. You could stay and find out for yourself… You could go and ask him, face-to-face."

"Oh, never. I could never do such a thing. What would he think of me, if such thoughts have never been in his mind?"

"But there's no one else. I told you what he said to

Miss Braithwaite. He doesn't love her. He said so clear as clear."

"Just because he doesn't love her, it doesn't necessarily mean he has…well, tender feelings for me. I'm sure that if he had, he would have found a way to tell me, in spite of all Miss Braithwaite's schemes."

"Papa is a very quiet person," Cecily said. "He doesn't do things rashly, or without thinking about them for a very long time. Perhaps he thinks you don't share his feelings."

Rosalind thought about this for a moment. "That's possible, I suppose, though I did think that I…well, never mind. I will recover from my disappointment while I'm abroad and when I return, I am sure we'll still be friends, will we not?"

"You're determined to go? You won't change your mind?" It was Cecily's turn to blink her eyes to stop herself from crying.

"I must… Kiss me goodbye, Cecily, and make sure to give Sam a hug from me."

"He'll be so sad…we both will."

"I know and so will I…but it can't be helped."

Rosalind went with Cecily to the front door. They clung together on the doorstep and then Cecily went down the steps to the street and started to walk home. Why hadn't Rosalind believed her? She was obviously not entirely persuaded that Miss Braithwaite had gone for ever…yes, that must be it. Why had Papa said nothing to her of his feelings? Really, he was too shy and you couldn't blame poor Rosalind for thinking as she did. Cecily was so distracted by her misery that she almost bumped into her father, who was striding swiftly in the opposite direction.

"Cecily?" he said. "Where have you been? You look quite pale and there are shadows under your eyes. Are you ill?"

"Papa! I've been to see Rosalind. She's going abroad. She's packing."

Papa left Cecily where she was in the middle of the pavement and began to run towards the Templeton house. Cecily followed, as quickly as she could and was in time to see him disappear inside. The sun was shining quite brightly and she decided to wait for him. She imagined the terrible scene that would be going on in the parlour. Rosalind would tell Papa she was going abroad. Would he be broken-hearted? How Cecily wished she had a father whose feelings were easier to guess at! He would probably come out looking crestfallen and sad and they'd go home together. She gathered her skirts about her and perched on the low wall with her back against the railings of the Templeton house. She was sure she wouldn't have long to wait.

Cecily was trying to write to Aunt Lizzie with Mossy lying curled up on her lap, which was rather trying. Nevertheless, she had to tell the story of what happened after she'd said goodbye to Rosalind.

I sat on the wall, she wrote, *for ever such a long time. I didn't dare go and knock on the door at the Templetons' again, so I went to see Amy and tell her and then we looked out of their front bedroom window for the rest of the afternoon. In the end, Papa and Rosalind came out together arm-in-arm and went off to the river. They are in love, Aunt Lizzie. Amy says so. They spend a great deal of time together and Rosalind comes to Number Six almost every day. Amy says Papa is out of practice because he hasn't been in love for the six years since Mama died.*

Cecily put down her pen and fell to stroking Mossy's back. She wouldn't tell Aunt Lizzie, and she hadn't yet told Amy, that she'd looked out of the nursery window last night, at twilight, and seen Papa and Rosalind kissing under the walnut tree. She and Sam might have a new mama after all. If there was to be a wedding, she would redecorate the doll's house in honour of the occasion. The *Willow* pattern wallpaper Rosalind had given her a few weeks ago lay in her chest of drawers and she would take it out and measure it for some of the main rooms. Cecily leaned her head on her hand and lost herself in happy daydreams, her letter unfinished on the table in front of her. Perhaps Rosalind would let her become a kind of apprentice and come sometimes to the studio where she worked. She would learn very quickly and soon she'd know enough to take every kind of photograph. "Ah yes, Miss Rosalind's young assistant," everyone would say. Cecily smiled to herself as she imagined the scene.

She moved her legs a little and startled Mossy, who jumped down and made for the door, with her tail held high.

"Goodbye, Mossy," Cecily said and then turned to write her letter again. *Can you keep a secret, Aunt Lizzie? Do not tell anyone, but I think Papa will soon ask Rosalind to marry him and we will have a new mama…*

Cecily had a vision of herself in a bridesmaid's dress taking off a pretty hat trimmed with roses and ribbons and lace, in order to cover her head with the black cloth again, ready to look through the lens and compose the perfect image of her papa and his new bride. She sucked the end of her pen and wrote: *If there*

is to be a wedding, I might be allowed to take some of the
pictures, for a bride cannot photograph herself, can she?
I hope so much that Rosalind will let me take her place
behind the camera on that day...

Then she wished her aunt an affectionate farewell,
signed the letter with her name, and added a whole
row of kisses.

Author's Note

·I was very happy to be asked to join Linda Newbery and Ann Turnbull in telling the stories of the inhabitants of Number 6, Chelsea Walk. This book is a close companion to *Girls with Courage*, sharing not only a setting but also some of the same characters.

I love the 1890s. I like the art, the literature and especially the theatre of those years and when I discovered that the first night of Oscar Wilde's *The Importance of Being Earnest* was on the 14th of February, I had a jumping-off point for my book.

I'm interested in photography. It's changed a lot since the 1890s. Everyone nowadays is fully equipped at all times with a camera in their smartphone. We take selfies, we photograph our lunch, we send pictures around the world on social media and think nothing of it. In the nineteenth century, things were vastly different but photography then was making enormous technological strides which led eventually to a time when everyone is a photographer.

I'm grateful to Angelo Hornak for guidance in technical matters and also to Laura Cecil for her help and advice.

It's been a pleasure to work with Linda and Ann and I'm grateful to Becky Walker for her help with this reissue. I'm really pleased that our books are reappearing in a lovely new format.

About the Author

Adèle Geras was born in Jerusalem and before the age of eleven had lived in Cyprus, Nigeria and North Borneo. She studied French and Spanish at Oxford University and taught French before becoming a full-time writer. She has written more than ninety books for children and young adults as well as six novels for adults.

She lives in Cambridge and has two daughters and four grandchildren.

To find out more about Adèle Geras, you can visit her website: www.adelegeras.com.

Discover more inspirational stories from
6 Chelsea Walk, and the girls who lived there
throughout history…

Girls for the Vote
1914
LINDA NEWBERY

When Polly discovers her new neighbours are suffragettes, fighting for women's right to vote, she is determined to join their protest march. But her parents are scandalized. Will she dare to defy them and do what she thinks is right?

Girls with a Voice
1764
ANN TURNBULL

Mary Ann's greatest wish is to become an opera singer, but when she is told she must leave her boarding school, her singing dreams are shattered. Distraught, she comes up with a plan to stay at school, oblivious to the danger it will put her in…

Girls behind the Camera
1895
ADÈLE GERAS

Cecily is enchanted when she meets Rosalind, a photographer, who seems to be the perfect match for Cecily's lonely widowed father. But her father's friend, the dull Miss Braithwaite, keeps spoiling her plans to unite the pair. Will Cecily's dreams ever come true?

Coming soon…

Girls with Courage
1857
ADÈLE GERAS

When Lizzie's stepfather sends her to stay with relatives in London, Lizzie struggles to adapt to her new life of stiff manners and formal pastimes. She lives for the daily letters from her mother, but when the letters suddenly stop, Lizzie sets out to discover the truth and finds herself on a rescue mission.

Girls on the Up
1969
LINDA NEWBERY

Andie dreams of becoming an artist and loves living in Chelsea, with the fashion, music and art galleries along the trendy King's Road. There's even a real artist living in the flat downstairs. Could Andie's paintings, inspired by the excitement of the first-ever moon landing, be good enough for her to achieve her dreams?

Girls at War
1941
ANN TURNBULL

When Josie goes to stay with her cousin, Edith, during the Blitz, she tries to fit in by joining Edith and her friends in teasing a timid classmate. But when the bullying gets out of hand, Josie faces a dilemma: she knows what it feels like to be picked on, but if she takes a stand, will Edith tell everyone her secret?

USBORNE QUICKLINKS

For links to websites where you can find out more about photography and famous artists in Cecily's time and learn about everyday life at the end of the Victorian age, go to the Usborne Quicklinks website at www.usborne.com/quicklinks and type in the title of this book.

At Usborne Quicklinks you can:

- See examples of Victorian photographs and daguerreotypes
- Take a tour of a Victorian home
- Examine Pre-Raphaelite and Impressionist paintings and find out about the artists
- See some of the fashions of the day

Please follow the online safety guidelines at the Usborne Quicklinks website.